TERIL'S FIRE

A MATE INDEX ROMANCE

S.J. SANDERS

*G*rish Ugaar was at a loss on how he might help his brother. Although assisting in a recent battle at the aid of their Arobi friends had lightened the male's spirits, it didn't last long. Before the first lunar cycle was complete, Borth had retreated once more into his private, pain-filled world. He would completely shut out even Grish on a bad day, when the agony from the ghosts of wounds he'd sustained on Agraadax overwhelmed him.

It was another bad day.

Even from halfway across the field, Grish could see the grimace on his brother's face. His right leg dragged with every movement, despite the supportive knee brace he wore to reinforce the cybernetic limb's ability to function under duress for long periods. On most days it did not bother him, but the rainy season was coming, and it seemed to irritate the phantom pains of wounds long since healed.

During the heat of the summer, it hadn't been so bad. Borth had even begun entertaining the idea of sending away for a mate, a small human who would not look down on the male for his physical inabilities.

That too, like so many things, was now relegated to a subject that his brother was in no mood to discuss.

That alone was frustrating. The medics said that half of Borth's problems weren't physical. If anyone needed a mate to distract him and shower him with love, affection, and approval, it was his brother. Humans weren't like Terils. They would never consider a Teril mate. Their refusal to mate with a female of their species had brought them to this world since they had avoided summons to return to their homeworld to be matched with an appropriate female.

Their species was too focused on physical strength and soundness of body for it to have been a healthy situation for Borth. A Teril was larger and stronger than most species in the Intergalactic Union. Weakness wasn't tolerated among their kind, and was not welcome among their females.

A human mate, however, would be different.

He knew he should have used their savings to acquire their female during the summer, before his brother's mood soured. He had hoped that things would last until the money from the harvest came in.

Now they were paying for that short-sightedness on his part.

It was for that reason that he was about to break his brother's trust and do something behind his back for the first time. He was going to order a mate for them from the Mate Index.

Clearing his throat, Grish raised his voice so to be heard.

"Borth, I'm going to the city to gather goods. I will be gone only overnight. Is there anything you want brought back?"

The only sign that his brother heard him was the hand the male raised to wave him off. He didn't look his way, nor call out lewd suggestions jovially as had been his custom.

His brother was broken. This, if nothing else, affirmed for him that he was doing what was right.

Humming to himself, he made his way to their flyer. He had

packed it earlier that day in preparation for the journey, so there was little to be done. Borth would amuse himself with vids as he nursed his pained leg, until hunger drove him to dig through their kitchen for food. Neither of them was much good at cooking, but they had a replicator that served its purpose. The irony wasn't lost on either of them that they were farmers selling crops to eat replicated food, but it was where they were.

Settling into the flyer, he could almost hear it creak from his weight. It was barely large enough for them. Their ganthli—the horned plating that fringed their heads—barely cleared the ceiling. No doubt once younglings began coming, they would have to invest credits into a larger flyer to serve their purposes. Grish smiled at the thought of having a family as he programmed the coordinates for the trading post.

Although it was a fair distance to the post, it was not only the sole place nearby to trade or buy supplies, but also one of the few long-range comm systems through which he would be able to attend the hologram meeting with the Mate Index representative.

He fingered the scrap that he had written the appointment on. He would have filed it on the comms, but everything was connected to the household comm, meaning Borth would have discovered his secret.

At the fourth hour past sunrise, he would make arrangements to begin their family. It was the very thing that had consumed his and Borth's thoughts since they formed their uthak.

A thrill ran through him as the flyer zipped through the air, and he shamelessly spent the flight mulling over what their mate might be like and how many offspring they would have. How soon and how often did human females prepare to breed, and how long was their gestation? These were unknowns to him, and he considered the many possible scenarios. He was so absorbed in his thoughts that he was somewhat surprised when the flyer came down at the rest lodge by the edge of post.

Heaving himself out of his chair, Grish pulled his pack from the storage compartment and walked with heavy steps toward the rest lodge, smaller citizens scurrying out of his way. Many were afraid of his species, and for good reason, but he found himself filled with a sudden apprehension that their mate might also be nervous or afraid around them. His mouth tightened, sending another citizen running for cover.

He would have to make sure to do everything in his power to make her comfortable. He would work extra hard at it to compensate for Borth's recent surliness.

Ducking into the low entrance of the lodge, he squinted down at the tiny local seated behind the counter. The male's eyes widened, and his head tipped back as he took in the whole of Grish's large frame.

The clerk swallowed nervously. "How long will you be staying?"

"Just one night," Grish replied. "I should have my supplies collected and my female underway to me before the end of the day."

"I… see," the male stated, his fingers nervously tapping at the large upright data screen in front of him. "Place your hand on the registry pad, please."

With a warm smile that for some reason made the male sink further into his chair, Grish lifted his hand and placed it on the pad. It flashed green, and the clerk gave him a tremulous smile.

"The locks to your room are now coded to you. Please go down the hall to room twelve."

Nodding in thanks, Grish turned away, adjusting his pack on his shoulder as he moved and made his way to his assigned room. As promised, the lock pad on the door recognized his handprint, and the door slid open before him.

It was just as nondescript as he remembered. Nothing but dull shades of sand hue. Still, it was serviceable. Leaving his pack on his bed, he left his room to find supplies for the rest of the day. Tomorrow, he wanted nothing to interrupt his appointment. He had heard that the officials for the Mate Index were notoriously difficult. Throughout the day, he wondered just how true the rumors were about the human officials, and it continued to plague his mind early in the morning when he set out to the transmitter.

Unfortunately, it all proved to be true.

Grish sat wedged onto a small chair as the holographic image of a stern human male leaned forward and inspected him critically, an out-of-date datapad clenched his hands.

"You say you're looking for a mate for you and your… brother." A faint look of distaste crossed the male's face so fast that a less observant male may have missed it. But not Grish.

The interview was already off to a bad start, it seemed. He did vaguely recall hearing that humans did not typically engage in such relationships that were common among other cultures in the Union. Grish cleared his throat and twitched with unease as he attempted to salvage the situation. He could not fail and have their application denied.

"We are not biological brothers, but brothers by uthak. It is the closest sort of brotherhood, one formed for creating family units. It is by our cultural traditions that we share a mate and work together to provide for the female and the rearing of offspring."

"And you plan to provide this by… farming," the human supplied, his brow knotting. "A strange occupation for males with a long history of enlistment."

"We are retired. Farming is an honorable pursuit for warriors. It keeps us active, something we require."

"And where is your brother?"

"Tending to the farm. It is difficult for us both to be away. There's always much work to be done."

The male made a noise in the back of his throat and nodded. His finger moved over the datapad as he no doubt skimmed over his application. An application that the male would have already read, but was making show of examining for the sake of performance. Humans had a flair of dramatic, as he already knew. Finally, the male set the application down and knitted his fingers together on the table before him.

"It seems your application is in order. Have you given any consideration to what sort of woman you're looking for as a mate?"

Grish stared blankly at the male. "I do not understand."

The human let out a nervous laugh. "Well, are you looking for a certain body type—curvy, athletic, slender—or perhaps a specific complexion or hair color?"

Humans really considered such things? Teril females would color and oil their scales, especially their horn crests, but never had he heard of anyone weighing the value of a mate on such things. Shrugging, he attempted a smile despite feeling less and less comfortable with the entire process.

He was doing this for their family. He would succeed!

"We have no preferences in such things. We just want a female who will be kind, loving, and patient. A good mate who will bring joy and comfort to our home. It would be an extra bonus if she's inquisitive and enjoy games of strategy. It will make passing time together pleasant, since we enjoy many games in the evenings as well as vids."

The human stared at him for a long moment, but then, to Grish's relief, the male suddenly smiled. It was not a pleasant smile, but there were worse.

"I believe I have a few options for you to consider. One in particular you might like. Very sweet disposition and clever. I'm certain you'll find her a good match."

Letting out a pent-up breath, Grish smiled and shifted in his seat with expectation.

Success!

CHAPTER 1

Crystal Inola Rivers frowned at the landscape. It was one of the circles of hell. She was sure of it. Nothing but rolling hillsides, grass, and dirt. It had to be a mistake. The view from the transport was so uninspiring that she turned to the captain and jabbed a finger toward the viewing screen.

"Are you *sure* this is it?"

"Yes. The coordinates indicate that this is Antari Minor."

"But there's nothing here!" she objected.

The enormous winged alien—an Itashvanda, she recalled—frowned as he squinted at the small town that looked like it wouldn't have been out of place on a Wild West set. She hated westerns.

"I disagree. There is quite clearly the trading port city, Intak-fell, exactly where we were instructed to take you."

Her heart sank. She was going to kill Robby if she ever saw him again.

Stupid fucking idiot.

For a fellow hacker, he had zero sense, especially since he had a tendency to use his skills for petty theft to feed his flash addiction when he was short on cash. The alien drug had arrived on

Earth five years ago and took the entire planet by storm. When he was wired on flash, he did stupid things—like try to steal from aliens.

She had told him to leave aliens alone, but when a large Calystii Imperial ship docked just outside the city, he was convinced he could get something worth selling. She wasn't sure what he stole, but knew that he had skipped town directly afterward, leaving a target on Crystal's back. She didn't have the opportunity to tell the Calystii that she didn't know what her idiot now-ex boyfriend did with the shit he stole.

The moment she returned to her apartment and found it ransacked with a warning scrawled across one wall that, thanks to her neurotranslator she had implanted just months earlier, she had been able to read, Crystal had skipped town. Sure, she could have stayed and tried to explain her innocence, but a warning to return said item or die horribly didn't inspire any confidence that they wouldn't torture or kill her regardless.

Unfortunately, the Calystii had been harder to shake than she thought they would be. They tracked her to every city she tried to hide out in, always coming dangerously close to capturing her. She wasn't sure what they had planned if they caught her. She was quite certain, however, that she didn't want to hang around and find out.

When she spotted the silvery males at the edge of a crowd during a rave, she knew she had to do something else. Datapad in hand, she had hacked into the Mate Index system, set up her account, and had it marked as approved and processed.

An alien world seemed like a better option for hiding.

So she thought, anyway.

But hiding out under the protective shadow of a burly alien who supposedly would worship the ground she walked on hadn't worked out too well. Every male she had been matched with sent her back to a Mate Index HQ on one of the various space stations within days of arrival.

She knew what her file said. That she was prickly, hostile, generally disagreeable about everything, antisocial, somber, frigid since she wouldn't drop panties and get to fucking, and unfeminine (listing her tattoos and piercings as being the worst taste for her sex), among other things. As if the guys she was sent to were any sort of prize. The last guy she was sent to, the Korovik, although he had been pretty, was a stuffy asshole with zero sense of humor. He hadn't appreciated it when she reprogrammed the entire household to make it more user friendly for her. He sent her back with an apologetic smile before she even had time to unpack as he informed her that they "just wouldn't suit."

Yeah. Sure.

That was the fifth time she was sent back. After that, it seemed that most males kept a wide berth from her. Normally she wouldn't cry over it, but she sure as hell didn't want to go back to Earth. Unfortunately, the asshole assigned to her case informed her that if she didn't make this mating work out that she was being sent back and permanently disqualified from entering the program again.

Not only that, but since they also caught on to her little trick, he had been pleased to inform her of the prison cell waiting for her on Earth if she didn't fulfill the terms of the contract she forged. Nice. They were willing to look the other way while there was a chance that she would do what she signed up for, but they were tired of losing funds due to dissatisfied males.

Crystal gently rolled her tongue piercing and scowled. At least she knew what the dick had been so happy about. This apparently was her punishment. It had to be. No one would consider sticking her there as any sort of favor toward her. She thrived off the urban vibe, the rush of city life and the electric information highways running through it day or night. A city rarely slept. A place where she could plug in and race among data highways.

What the fuck was she going to do here?

A loud sigh escaped her as she turned to glance over at her escort again. "Please tell me that this is just a little out of the way place, and that there are at least some kind of cities around."

It was foolish to cling to hope, especially when that very quality had been what kept her with Robby when she should have cut him loose, but she tried to be optimistic that there was something she could salvage out of the situation. That hope was dashed when the alien shook his head, his enormous leathery wings shifting behind him.

"Antari Minor is an outer planet, the settlements forming around farming and mining communities. Intakfell is one of the largest trading ports on the continent."

"With the way my luck has been, it figures you'd say something like that," she replied as she squinted at the town.

Despite the starships and private flyers docked everywhere just outside the town, the trading port itself was dreary. The scattered buildings were all made of the cheap, bland insta-structure material that was used throughout the Intergalactic Union for setting up inexpensive buildings. Earth had bought a bunch of it to work toward dealing with the homeless population, but she understood that its wider use was in starting the basic structures for new colonies.

These, however, looked as if they had been used far longer than they were designed to be. The material still held together, but it was badly abraded from weather. That told her that they had been there longer than the hundred or so years that they were meant to be used for. She didn't even want to think about the numerous questionable stains that appeared along the lower walls. No doubt some of it was food, but the rest... she wasn't going there. A pair of droids exited a nearby building, nearly as worn in appearance as the town.

"I'm in a high-tech version of an old shanty town," she muttered to herself with a shudder.

"Do you find the planet objectionable?" the Itashvanda asked curiously.

"Only if you consider Tatooine minus the desert objectionable," she replied. "For me, that would be a resounding yes."

"Ah… a lack of deserts. If it is any comfort to you, there is desert on approximately forty-eight percent of this planet's surface. Those zones are generally uninhabitable, save for some species of crops that thrive in such climates. If you are fortunate, your mate may be in one of those zones. The file just says that he is a farmer by name of Grish Ugaar."

A farmer. She was going to be spending what may be the rest of her life with a farmer—possibly on a farm in desert conditions in the middle of nowhere.

"Fucking perfect," she sighed.

The Itashvanda smiled. "I am glad I could be of assistance to alleviate your concerns."

Crystal stared at him blankly. *Did he…?* He did. He actually thought he had helped her. It was on the tip of her tongue to tell him that it didn't alleviate her concerns and in fact did the opposite, but despite being somewhat unscrupulous at times, she was burdened with a soft heart. So instead, she returned his smile as she held back the pained grimace that threatened to pull at her mouth.

"I hope that this does not offend you, but you do not look like the other brides we have transported," he observed, his brow puckering a little as he glanced over her attire.

Squashing a derisive laugh, Crystal's smile widened. "No, I suppose I don't."

On her first matched mating, she saw how many of the brides

were dressed when arriving at port. The majority of the women had dressed… well, like brides. With her messy ponytail, scuffed sneakers, an oversized band shirt, and her best pair of black leggings, she knew she didn't make the perfect picture of a blushing bride eagerly awaiting her mate. She didn't even have a splash of lipstick since she didn't own any makeup—well, none she had remembered to throw into her Bug Out Bag. Not that there was space for her to fit much. There had only been enough room for her to toss in a few changes of leggings and several tees. When running for one's life, comfort and utility over fashion seemed like the wiser choice. At that time, she hadn't considered that she would need to escape Earth.

Watching her matched mate look right past her, hoping that one of the well-dressed manicured women was his, had stung. When he finally realized that *she* was his, the disappointment on his face had been acute, evident in every useless salon appointment he booked and every ugly, uncomfortable outfit he insisted she wear in his presence. Of course, she hadn't been welcome to take any of the clothes with her, and she was glad because she hadn't wanted to deal with getting rid of it.

Any hope that her next mate would be better died a swift death upon meeting her second match. Thankfully, it hurt a little less each time it happened so that now, with the Itashvanda looking at her clothes doubtfully, she barely felt anything more than wry amusement.

"I'm afraid when I left Earth, I packed for comfort and didn't really think ahead to the arrival."

He nodded and patted her arm reassuringly. "Do not worry, female. A good male will see the value of a mate regardless of her odd apparel."

She wanted so badly to snort derisively at that but opted instead for returning to people-watching as the crowds moved to and from the large market. Crystal shifted uneasily. The mash of numerous species was chaos, but as she watched them, she wondered, like the Old West of Earth, just how much lawlessness was on Antari Minor. Sure, she often stepped on the wrong side of the law, but she had never physically hurt someone. Even hacking, she only took jobs that targeted entities who could afford the hit and deserved it. The idea of being thrown alongside possible killers and hardened criminals outside of her usual crowd was making her increasingly nervous.

"So," she began, "what do you know of this place other than geography? Is it pretty safe usually?"

The male tilted his head in consideration. "It is widely known that the planet harbors intergalactic criminals, but also that most of the males who come to lose themselves here are doing so to escape that life, so few bother them. There are always those who might hide out here to shake the law, but nothing escapes the notice of locals. In that way, it can be considered safer than many other places, although like most things, it can be a matter of perspective."

"I see," she murmured.

It wasn't entirely comforting, but it was better than she feared. There was *some* sort of law and order, even if it came from retired killers keeping the others in line to some degree. At least there was a lower chance of someone running wild, threatening to cut her life short. If she wanted that, she could have remained on Earth running from the Calystii. It sounded like those thugs would have a harder time running loose on Antari Minor, and that cheered her some.

"Any idea when he's coming?"

"Your mate responded to our comms upon landing and indicated that he was en route to the trading port. He will be here soon."

The Itashvanda shifted uncomfortably, drawing her attention.

"What's wrong?"

The male's gray skin acquired a bluish flush, his dark crest of leathery feather things flattening to his head with discomfort.

"I did not wish to bring up the subject, but as he is on his way and we are running behind to our next destination on our route…"

They were anxious to be on their way, and she wasn't their problem. Of course they wanted to be on their way. No doubt they preferred to just dump her out there and leave as fast as possible to move on to their next item of business. That was all it was—business. She was cargo. She was going to be in Intakfell alone.

Crystal felt a trickle of fear but pushed it back. She was twenty-nine years old. She had a lot of time since becoming an adult of being on her own. Never on an alien world, but she would handle it.

"I get it," she said, softening the sharp bite of her words with a small smile. "If he'll be arriving soon, there's no reason for you to just hang around and babysit me in a place that ought to be relatively safe."

The male let out a relieved sigh and smiled down her. "Precisely. I would recommend that you wait in the teahouse. Best to stay clear of the activity in the market since you have a lot of offworld traffic there. The proprietress of the teahouse will make certain no one disturbs you while you wait. I will personally comm your mate so that he knows where to collect you and make certain that the owner of the teahouse is available to greet you."

"Thank you," she murmured, grateful in face of the uncharitable thought she had just moments before.

Since she didn't have any personal possessions with her other than the small bag she wore over one shoulder, it didn't take long before she was on the ground making her way toward the teahouse. At her approach, a door slid open, revealing a muted interior with a spicy-sweet scent that ran over her senses like honey and cinnamon. Although it wasn't an exact fit, it was familiar enough that it sent a wave of unexpected homesickness through her.

Blinking several times, she stayed rooted in place as she allowed her eyes to adjust to the dim interior. Swathes of beautiful fabric fell, segmenting the larger room into smaller, semi-private areas as males and females alike sat on plush pillows around circular tables as they spoke, stopping only to sip tea from brilliantly painted heavy glass cups. A few eyes turned her way , but it was only in passing curiosity. Most ignored her presence, engaged in conversation, drink, and in a few cases smoking from long, thin, hooked pipes.

From one corner of the room, a large female covered in pale golden scales bustled forward, her shrewd green eyes focused on Crystal before a wide smile broke out over her face. The darker golden brown braids of her hair fell over her shoulders, the ends swaying gracefully with every step. She wore a sleeveless red robe with wide slits on the sides beneath her arms to accommodate her folded wings.

"You are Crystal, yes?" the female's soft, raspy voice addressed her.

Crystal nodded, clutching her small bag closer to her. "Yes."

"I thought so. We do not see many of your species around here. I was asked to see to your comfort while you wait for your mate. In the meantime, I am Nikana. Welcome to my teahouse. I have all the best teas from Mora II. We Morith are known best for it, so you are in for a treat." She paused, a tiny frown puckering her brow. "You do like tea, don't you?"

"Yes," Crystal lied.

"Wonderful! What is your preference? Something light and floral, sweet with a hint of rich flavor?"

"How about bold, dark, and packs a punch?" Crystal asked.

Nikana blinked slowly before a low chuckle burst from her. "I see you are a customer after my own heart. You sit here," she said gesturing to a small table, "and I will get for you intimbar."

Crystal settled among her pillows, eyeing the other patrons until the proprietress returned with another thick glass in hand, this one a bit larger, with dark, steamy liquid in it. A bitter aroma hit her nose, suffused with spices like some sort of fancy seasonal flavoring. As the cup was set in front of her, she bit back her instinctive request for creamer and cradled it in her hands. Asking for dairy was hazardous among aliens.

At best, it earned an odd look as the alien tried to wrap their mind around the fact that someone actually wanted to consume that. At worst, the milk source was so strange that she couldn't stomach the thought of drinking it. That one she found out the hard way, with failed match number two, who offered her the pulverized innards of a huge, monstrous worm he had discerned to be their closest equivalent to milk.

She learned her lesson there.

Bringing the cup up to her lips, fully conscious of Nikana's eyes on her, she took a small sip and bit back an exclamation of surprise as the dark liquid hit her tongue. Instead, she let out a loud, embarrassing moan and took a deeper sip. It was like coffee, cream, dark chocolate, and a dash of cinnamon in the slightly sweet drink. It was indeed rich, bold, and dark and satisfied every craving she had had for months.

Suddenly, every eye in the tea house was on her, but one pair in particular felt heavy. That gaze grew even weightier as everyone turned to look in that direction.

Nikana's eyes sparkled, and she chuckled. That alone was finally what broke the frozen hold over her muscles. Slowly, she raised her eyes, and they fastened on the largest male she had ever seen in her life.

Just over what had to be seven and a half feet tall, positively dwarfing her five feet and six inch frame, the enormous male was a dark sandy brown, the scales on his body thick like a crocodile all the way from his head to the end of the thick tail swaying behind him, and yet they possessed a suppleness in places that drew her eyes. Flushing when she discovered that she was staring at the expanse of muscle peeking out from his shirt, she lifted her gaze to his face.

Every line was strong and blunt, with small horns studding the length of his jaw and over his eyes, and even larger horns rising from a thick, boney crown-like crest. Every inch of him was hard and rugged. So much so that he looked like he could beat the Kool-Aid man in a wall-breaking contest. There was something so primitive and undeniably appealing about him despite his obvious alienness. Even his blunt, flattened nose seemed to fit him perfectly.

Crystal took a hasty sip in a vain effort to distract herself from the muscle lover's buffet in front of her. She was as good as mated. She should at least try to act appropriately so she didn't get sent back by yet another male.

"Ah, Grish!" Nikana exclaimed with a happy greeting. "I see you have arrived in time to enjoy some intimbar with your new mate!"

Him? He was her mate?

Crystal felt a bit light-headed, possibly from all the blood rushing to her head with the blush deepening on her cheeks. She cursed her light Cuban complexion as he came to a stop in front of her, his eyes fastening on her.

"You are Crystal?" he rasped.

"Yes."

Was that her voice sounding all breathless and husky as his gaze practically devoured her? That chemistry hadn't been there with the other matches. This arranged mate just might work out. Just maybe the universe was going to cut her a break for once.

He made a rumbling sound of approval as his eyes roamed

over her before fixing on her face. He peered at her for a long moment.

"What is that metal deformity on your nose?" he asked.

"It's *not* a deformity," she snapped.

She was aware of her neck growing hot with the attention of everyone in the teahouse on them. A soft laughter rose from somewhere behind her, deepening her embarrassment. It appeared that the universe still had jokes.

CHAPTER 2

"My nose piercing is ornamental," his mate hissed. "At the moment, however, I'm trying to figure what purpose those monstrosities you call your horns serve other than to drain power from your brain."

Grish started, perplexed at the vehemence in her voice until he realized what he had done. He had embarrassed his mate. He wanted to groan. He did not know what had come over him. He had seen the strange metal bit protruding from the side of her nose and had been caught by surprise. Mortification suffused his mate's round, soft cheeks, and a spark of anger lit her dark blue eyes.

For a second, he was caught in her gaze. Her eyes were like the deepest of pools, ringed in an even darker shade of blue. A color that seemed to deepen with her mounting anger. He had just met his mate, and he had already managed to offend her. Borth would never let him live it down if he found out. Desperately, he sought some way to remedy it.

"Not that it is unattractive. Odd growths can have a certain charm on the right female. My mother, in fact…"

"Please... *please*, sit down and shut up," she choked out around her fury, her teeth audibly grinding together.

That could not be a good sign.

Though the words were spoken so softly that he barely heard them, he sank his enormous girth to the cushions on the other side of her, taking care to not accidentally hit her legs with his tail, and shut his mouth so fast that his teeth clicked together.

"My apologies," he muttered. "I did not mean to embarrass you. I have not seen a female adorn herself in such a way before. I honestly have not had such an unfortunate encounter with a female since my youth."

To his relief, a bit of the tension eased from her, and she regarded him skeptically, one peculiar human eyebrow raised in his direction. "Are you trying to tell me that you're normally some kind of Casanova?"

He snapped his fingers and let out a booming bark of laughter. "I know that reference! The humans in my squad used it many times. That wouldn't be an accurate descriptor, no. But neither have I failed to communicate so horribly. I thought I left that behind... when I was an awkward youngling."

To his surprise, a smile appeared on her full, inviting lips as she visibly thawed a little and settled more comfortably. He wasn't sure how much of it was to lead him into a false sense of security, so he kept his full attention on her, as if she were a dangerous pit marslet rather than a tiny human.

"Just how awkward?" she asked.

He grinned at the memory. "My brain-draining horns you were admiring were far too large for my frame, and my tail was still on the stubby side. I was all wiry muscle and large hands, horns, and feet, and had a penchant for speaking before what I said made any contact with my brain. My mother, many times, marveled that I survived to adulthood. Though one thing remains the same."

A soft chuckle escaped his female, bringing a surge of warmth to his heart.

"Good to know the awkward stage isn't unique to humans. My hair and skin were oily, and I already had bigger boobs than any girl my age. I was frequently the butt of jokes carried out by adolescent boys. I'm so glad those years are behind me."

"Not all Terils suffer so unfortunately, but we do have an ungainly phase that we must suffer through," he agreed, sitting back as he poured the intimbar into his own cup. Taking a deep, satisfying sip, he rumbled with pleasure. "Intimbar, one of the greatest of delights from Mora II."

"It is good," Crystal agreed. "Like coffee with other stuff added."

It was probably not polite, but Grish could not restrain the laughter that boomed from him. His little female would hopefully forgive him. "I have had this human coffee through the replicator. It is not bad, but it is weak and bland compared to intimbar."

Crystal's laughter stirred in response, and she regarded him through eyes slit with mirth. "You're basing human coffee on what you get through a replicator? That's crazy. Coffee carries a personality that depends on who's making it. It varies not only from household to household but between cultures. If I had some decent roasted beans, I'd make you coffee like my *abuela* made."

The note of challenge in her voice made him smile.

"Very well, *katna*. I have a connection with a trader who brings me supplies. I am certain he can acquire your coffee. You will have your opportunity to prove it to me. Speaking of home," he sighed as he tossed back the rest of the intimbar in his cup, "we should be going. It is a long flight home, and even leaving now, it will be quite late by the time we return."

He did not look forward to how Borth would receive their arrival well after dark fall. He still had not informed his brother that he was bringing home a female. He had merely made his excuses about needing to pick up a delivery. That was not quite a lie.

Lie or not, Borth wasn't going to be pleased. Hopefully, he would not be angered too long.

Crystal hurriedly drank her own intimbar and stood. She was so small next to him that he faltered for a moment. She was not quite as short as the Arobi's human mate, but next to him, he was aware of just how delicate she was compared to himself. Perhaps he should have been more specific and asked for a tall female…

No, despite how small and vulnerable she was, he already could not imagine replacing her with another female.

She didn't say anything as she followed him to the flyer, her lips pinched tight with uncertainty. Poor female had to be nervous. This was an entirely new world, and now she was mated as well.

"This must all be very new for you," he said conversationally.

She glanced up at him, her brows drawing up. "Didn't they tell you… No, not too different. I mean, the planet is a surprise, to say the least. But the situation itself is not. I've been sent to five other males on four different planets and one space station. I'm afraid whoever handled your case neglected to tell you that you were getting a rejected mate."

Despite her careless grin, Grish heard the pain in her voice. Her other matched mates had thrown her away. He bit back a growl and attempted to regain control of his anger on her behalf before he said anything he would regret. He didn't want to alarm her with the protective instincts already surging through him that demanded that he challenge each of the males who had hurt her. He gave her what he hoped was a charming smile as he spoke.

"All the better that the males were foolish enough to part with you. They obviously weren't the sort to appreciate a female and wisely left you for a male who could."

One corner of her mouth quirked upward. "That is really sweet. Nicely done."

"Bah, nothing nicely done about it when words are spoken in sincerity," he replied with a snort of distaste. "You should know: Terils as a species do not flatter. We are fond of a good joke or boast, but false compliments are considered beneath us, an insult to the individual falsely praised. I would not so insult you."

Her lips parted in an expression of surprise before her mouth slowly closed. She gave a small thoughtful huff and shook her head. "Of all the things I've heard over the years, *that* is actually a new one for me."

Grish's smile widened into a flirtatious grin as he activated the security locks on the flyer and stepped aside to allow the ramp to descend.

"You will learn many new, interesting things with Teril mates."

The laughter that burst from her was genuine and full, her body shaking with it as her eyes teared. She was a joyous sight. Watching her amusement, he was certain that he was half in love with her already.

Gesturing for her to precede him up the ramp, he followed his small mate inside the flyer. Unlike the cramped conditions that he and his brother dealt with, watching Crystal walk to the flight console, he was aware of just how little space she took up in the vessel. Taking a seat in the navigation station, she gave him an uncertain look as he dropped into the pilot seat beside her.

"This is all... very big," she observed as he input the flight coordinates.

"We are a big species," he replied. "It is overwhelming, I know, but we will do all we can to make you comfortable. Starting with this."

With a flourish, he pulled out a food storage container and unlocked it, the escaping cold air blowing across his face.

"It is cold, but cold veriksnal is good. I hope you enjoy it, *katna*."

Crystal gave him a grateful look as she leaned forward and reached in to grab several strips of cold-stored veriksnal meat.

"Thank you," she murmured.

Settling back once more, she began to eat, a sound of surprised pleasure escaping her at the first taste. Other than that little sound, they shared their meal together in silence, but Grish felt a deep satisfaction that he had provided well for his mate.

Although he tried to keep himself occupied with his meal and with the controls of the flyer so as to not overwhelm her with too much of his company too soon, he found himself glancing at her as he mentally went over how he might proceed to win her affections. So far, he didn't have much other than to *not* smother her, as his human friends advised when he sought them for advice. Hayley, the kind female mated to his Arobi friends, however, told him to be upfront with his desire and interest to avoid any misunderstandings.

Be direct, but not overwhelming.

He prayed he wouldn't make a disaster of it.

Hours passed, during which she drifted in and out of sleep. It wasn't until they were approaching the farm that she roused herself and stretched. Squinting at the dark landscape lit only by the beams of the flyer, she sighed and shifted in her chair as he began their descent.

Darting a curious glance his way, she cleared her throat. "Tell me, what sort of tech connection do you have at the farm?"

Startled, Grish glanced down at her. His tiny human was inquiring about tech connections? He eased and laughed silently to himself. She must be worried that she would not have access to vids. He understood that humans enjoy their many entertainments.

"We do have a long-distance comm. Though it's not a wide-range intergalactic class that will allow you to comm Earth directly, we do have access to vids and long-distance contact with some of the neighboring systems," he informed her as he began the landing procedures.

"So I can link into the intergalactic data systems from your farm?" she asked, her eyes glittering with something fiercer than excitement, not even taking note of the subtle jerk of the flyer as it settled on the landing pad outside the domicile.

"We may have to do some upgrades for full uplink ability," he said slowly as he unbelted himself and stood, still uncertain what she would need it for, "but it would be easy enough."

Her face fell in disappointment, but she summoned up a strained smile as she also unstrapped and followed him to the exit port. "But not yet, huh? Out of curiosity, how long do the upgrades take?"

Grish pursed his lips as he stopped in front of the door and considered. "I would have to comm a trader to bring the materials I would need and set up an account with the intergalactic server… Six lunar cycles, seven at maximum."

"Six or seven months…" she whispered. Her smile wobbled, and she appeared to stiffen her spine as if facing an adversary. It was fascinating to watch. "Sounds great. I really appreciate all the effort you're willing to go through."

"A small effort for the happiness of our mate," he soothed as he took her hand and led her out of the flyer.

She halted the moment her feet hit the solid turf, confusion clouding her expression.

"Our?"

"My brother and me. You are our mate."

Her mouth dropped open, her eyes wide with shock. He wanted to soothe her, but the door of the domicile slammed open at that moment, light flooding over them.

"Grish, you're back. I was wondering what was taking you so… What in Engril's name is *that* doing here?"

"Excuse me? What the fuck do you mean by *that*?" Crystal snarled. She glared at Borth before turning a hard look back to him. "And again, what's this 'our' bullshit? I don't do multiple mates."

"In this case, you will not be," Borth replied tersely. "Get her off our property now."

CHAPTER 3

Crystal stared at the pale straw-colored Teril—supposedly her other mate—who had come from the house. Horror at the idea of being match mated to two huge males had been eclipsed by outrage at how he reacted to her presence and a very real fear that if Grish did exactly as his brother demanded, she would be returned to Earth.

Do not pass Go. Do not collect two hundred dollars. She would be heading straight to jail.

While at least there she would be safe from the Calystii, she hardly wanted to face a prison sentence for fraud, hacking, and a slew of other charges that the Mate Index legal team would manufacture. And unlike other women in the system, who were given a chance to start over through the Mate Index, she would no longer be eligible for that opportunity.

She would have nothing to look forward to but many years in a prison cell.

That was the one thing that gave her a pause and kept her from lashing out at being called "that." Without that threat hanging over her head, she might have taken Borth at his word, told him to shove it, and demanded that Grish take her back into town.

Clenching her jaw, she met his irate gaze with a hard glower. She wasn't going to flip out on his ass, but she wasn't going to let him to think that was acceptable either.

"Not so fast, asshole. Despite the fact that I'm still trying to process here—because really, who the hell shares a mate with their brother?—I am not leaving just because you say so. Grish here has a contract with the Mate Index. He's the only one who can ask me to leave. Furthermore," she swallowed as she took a small breath, preparing to lie her ass off, "my contract obligates him to eight months minimum before he can terminate the contract."

Grish looked at her, his expression blank. She wasn't sure if he knew that she was lying, but if he did, he didn't let on to Borth. Instead, he shrugged.

"Ah, if eight months it must be, then eight months it is. There is nothing to be done about it, Borth," he said with all appearance of being apologetic to his brother.

"No need to look so cheerful," the other male snapped, his scales darkening with his increasing fury.

Grish turned to her with a helpless look. "It seems I have erroneously angered my brother. As there's little I can do to remedy it, I may at least set your mind at ease and inform you that we are not brothers by blood. There are some species who have evolved that way, such as the Edoka, but not the Teril. It seems the agent did not give you all the details either. I gave all the information regarding our culture and family unit to him. In our culture, males pair into uthaks to form a family unit with a female."

"Information that you do not need to know because it's not happening," Borth bit out, directing a scathing look at his brother, though his words were directed at her. When his eyes turned to her once more, the deep amber-red seemed almost ready to shoot flames from their depths. He was *really* angry. "I do not want a female here. Not you, not any female. The moment we are able to, we will be returning you to the Mate Index Distribution Program. Grish should never have sent for you."

"Yeah… well, unfortunately, he did. So now we all get to play nice for the next few months," she bluffed, adopting a sharp tone that didn't require much acting on her part.

He was starting to piss her off. Yeah, he wasn't happy. She got that. This wasn't a picnic for her either, and it certainly wasn't what she had asked for on her forged application, but she was adjusting. Given time, she could have become comfortable with the arrangement. But that wasn't likely to happen.

Grish was a nice guy, and she hated to lead him on and take advantage of him, but she didn't see her and Borth coming around. Once again, she needed to look out for herself, even if being the cream filling in their enormous sex cookie was equally fascinating and terrifying.

No, her days were obviously numbered, and she would need to take advantage of what little of it she would have to link into the intergalactic data streams, find a way to earn credits, and establish contacts.

Borth squinted at her, and she adopted a bored expression, giving away nothing. Finally, he grunted and turned away from her, his gait stiff.

"Very well. If we must endure the company of the female, then there's nothing more I can do. Fair warning, brother: I will not be waiting on her or indulging her," Borth grumbled. "She is not my mate. You brought her here—you deal with her and keep her out of my way until you can return her."

Grish gave her an apologetic look as the other male made his exit, his long tail slashing behind him. "He's not usually so irritable. It is late and he worked in the fields all day. No doubt his leg is bothering him. It will be better in the morning."

It wasn't better in the morning.

Oh, Borth didn't direct any more scathing observations or comments in her direction. He didn't say anything at all to her. Instead, he acted as if she wasn't there. His attention was entirely on the morning meal that he prepared for himself, leaving Grish to show her where the replicator was and familiarize her with the menu program. After he was certain that she had it, he retrieved the food he had selected for himself and went to sit beside Borth.

Crystal frowned at the unappealing selections. There were variations of boiled grains and protein-laden stews of unidentifiable ingredients. Nothing looked close to what she would consider edible. Was this the crap they were living on? Why when they had such a large, well-equipped kitchen? They were farmers, for fuck's sake. She was still trying to decide what she wanted when the males pushed back their chairs and stood.

She had only been looking over the selections for a few minutes, and they were already done! She watched in surprise as they carried their dishes to the dish sanitation unit and neatly put them inside without a word. It was such an obvious routine that she almost felt sorry for just how staid their lives, going through the motions in the morning as they prepared to go out into the fields. It was efficient, sure, but it was all so stiff and practiced that it didn't seem at all like a couple of guys comfortable in their own home, getting ready for the day.

Borth didn't look her way as he walked by her, his massive body moving with almost soundless grace despite his size and the supportive brace around his knee. Grish followed close behind him but stopped when he reached her side. He seemed disconcerted that she had yet to eat and gave her a worried glance.

"You should eat something, *katna*."

She grimaced and made an uncomplimentary grunt at the idea.

"I will. It's just hard to choose."

He gave her a doubtful look but nodded.

"Good. Eat and rest today. I will be back to check on you at midday."

Hours of nothing to do to occupy herself in an empty farmhouse. *Let the good times roll.*

Sighing, she eyed him, reluctant for him to leave. "Why do you call me that?"

"It is a term of endearment that males enjoy calling their mates," he answered with an easy smile.

"I think your brother would disagree with that usage."

"As you say, he has eight lunar cycles to get used to the idea," Grish laughed.

One large hand ruffled her shoulder-length hair before he too left, following his brother out.

"Be sure to eat something!" he yelled back just as he stepped outside of the dwelling, the door sealing behind him.

Sighing, she looked back at the display menu again. Boiled grain snot with questionable fruit topping it was. At least she *hoped* that was fruit.

It wasn't fruit. It was some sort of red sponge cake-like bits mixed in with the gruel, obviously intended to sweeten and provide some texture. The first bite made her instinctively gag as the mush coated her tongue. She wondered if the plain grain snot would have been easier to consume. The taste wasn't so horrible if one could get beyond the texture. For Crystal, there was no going beyond it. But half a lifetime of her *mamá* telling her not to be wasteful meant that she choked down every bite.

With that ordeal endured, Crystal put her bowl with those of the Ugaar brothers and set about exploring. She didn't know shit about what needed to be maintained around a farmhouse, but it definitely wasn't cleaning. She was nearly run down by a hip-high droid that powered through the entrance into the kitchen.

She watched after it for a moment before continuing on her way farther into the house, taking a left at the fork in the hallway just outside the kitchen. A quick investigation revealed that the entire place was clean to a point near unattainable for human standards by several roaming droids of various sizes.

The house was pretty unremarkable. There was a cleansing unit, one large bedroom and four others. She wondered if the "brothers" shared the large room intended for them and their mate or if they spread out among the rooms. Her room had been vacant, but there was more than enough space for them each to have a room or two for their own use. She peeked into each one, unsurprised to find every room immaculate.

If she wasn't mistaken, they were not staying together in the larger room, but neither did they have many belongings to give a true sense of having a presence in their rooms. As someone who always vigorously marked out her territory with photos and color that made a statement of who she was, the emptiness of their rooms disturbed her on a personal level. Who didn't surround themselves with beautiful things and little mementos of cherished memories?

Frowning, she stepped back out into the hallway and looked at the blank walls with a critical eye. Not a picture or a single work of art or spiritual homage. Nothing around her gave her any sense of the brothers.

Having gone as far as she could, she turned around and traced her steps back through the hall, passing the kitchen once more until she arrived at a large room. The first sign of character was an enormous stuffed couch that sat in the middle of the room, turned to face one wall.

There were no armrests. Rather, the high back seemed to frame all three sides with thick padding that looked comfortable to lean upon. The material a dark charcoal gray, it appeared soft and inviting. As she approached, the viewscreen taking up the entirety of one wall blinked on, startling her. The light blue screen flashed in waiting mode while she collected her thoughts. This was a newer model than anything she had on Earth, though she knew at least one of her previous mates had something similar. Seldom did she have the freedom to access one before she was sent back.

"Cycle up one click," she commanded.

The image of a scowling Calystii male had her stumbling back in shock until the camera panned away to show more of the scene. The male was scowling down at a female sobbing on her knees as she stretched her arms out to him.

What in the world...? Did aliens have soap operas?

Like staring at a train wreck, she slid forward, watching as the female sobbed and begged the male not leave, reaching for him as he stared down at her dispassionately. A large Lorgor male stood just behind him, waiting for any order that the male who was his obvious employer might give.

Crystal slid onto the couch, eyes wide as the drama continued to play out. The female pleaded with the male not to take another mate, to think of their younglings and everything she had done for him to help him acquire his position. She gripped his leg as he made to move, but he shook her off, leaving her sobbing, crumpling to the floor as he walked away with orders to the Lorgor to deal with her.

Throwing up an arm at the screen in outrage, Crystal made a sound of pure disgust in her throat. "What are you doing? Don't sit there and cry. At least take off one of the monstrosities clinging to your feet and chuck it at him. His face is far too pretty, anyway!"

Nestled on the couch, she muttered about spineless females just as the Lorgor leaned down to grab her, hauling her to her feet. He purred something in a low, inaudible voice, but whatever it was outraged the female so much that she struck out at him violently.

The male ducked away, his hand coming up to grip her arm

just as the camera zoomed in on his stern, unyielding face. That didn't stop her. The doormat came alive as she spat at him, hissing all manner of vile things and insulting his parentage even as she appeared to smolder up at him as he leaned down closer.

Crystal cackled, drawing her legs up beside her as she snuggled down against the thick padding of the cushion, mourning her lack of snacks.

orth scowled in the direction of their domicile. "You should have told me what you had planned."

"And you would have said no," Grish replied with his usual calm candor.

His brother wasn't wrong on that. He did not want a mate, not yet. He did not want a female to see him as he had become—to pity him. That would be as bad as the condemnation that would come from their own species. He had felt so much better weeks earlier, and now, as the harvest season cycled around, his body was beginning to betray him again.

"Why do you not understand that I do not want a female to see me like this?" he growled angrily.

"I do understand it, but I also understand that we have to face facts that it might not get better. You may continue to have problems during the wet season, and the misery you sink into every revolution isn't good for you or for our uthak."

His brother may have had a point, but it wasn't one he wished to consider yet. He did not want to entertain the fact that there might be no full recovery as the medics had warned. So many males were able to transition to replacement limbs easily. The trauma to his wounds was deeper, stretching out many days before he could be properly seen to by medics. He did not blame the Agraak healers who saved him. They had done the best that they could. He just did not want to believe that his life was going to be so different and he would no longer be able to depend on the strength he had all his life.

What was Borth Ugaar without his strength? Not a warrior nor a suitable mate. He couldn't suitably defend and provide for a female in the way their traditions dictated. He steeled himself against the pain that attempted to swallow him. She had been a pretty little female too…

"She is too small," he muttered resentfully.

Grish sighed. "I like her size. She would be sweet to snuggle against during the cold nights of winter."

"You expect that little female to warm you?" Borth asked in disbelief.

"I believe that she has enough fire in her to heat my blankets, among other things," Grish returned with a grin.

Borth wished that he could laugh and jest back, imagining the tiny female curled up protectively between them. Yet he had no laughter, and the image forged a painful lump in his throat.

"You do realize it will be nearly spring before we can get rid of her," Borth muttered, glaring down at the machinery that sat between them. "I hope with all this blanket heating, you do not get attached. We are not keeping her, Grish."

"I hear your words, brother."

"And proceed to release them out of the other ear," he snorted.

Grish laughed, shoving his arm playfully. Borth's knee twinged, but it was still early in the day and it did not complain more than that, nor did it threaten to buckle beneath him. He growled back, a deep rolling sound that exited the vibration passages on his ganthli, making a hollow thunderous sound.

Above, the skies answered with a growl, making them both

fall silent, their heads falling back to watch as dark clouds rolled through the air. The thunder roared again, but that time it was followed by a flicker and crack of lightning.

Borth sighed and returned his glare to the machine.

"We have paid many credits for this harvester and have not been able to use it yet," he grumbled as he activated its protective seal-lock and watched as the barrier folded up from its sides to snap around it.

Grish shrugged. "We will get our chance. We have a few weeks' window to get the harvest done. The storms are but a small delay."

"We have had more than our share of delays."

"Two storms back to back… This makes three. That is not too terrible," Grish argued cheerfully. "I was told of a revolution where it rained for two lunar cycles, flooding the farmlands, and the males had only a week to accomplish the harvest before the crops rotted. They survived that. We will survive this."

"You are disgustingly cheerful today," Borth observed moodily.

"A new mate makes it hard to be petulant about anything," his brother replied. "You should try it. Let yourself enjoy her company and these worries will seem small and insignificant. She is hope and the future for us, brother."

"Perhaps once that would have been the case, but there is no future with my leg the way it is. You should have allowed me to release you from the uthak. Then you would have been free to join with another male to welcome a mate."

The words soured in his belly, but it was only right to remind his brother that he still had a choice. A better male would secure their female, not frighten her away with his crippling pain and bad attitude. Turning away from the machine, he headed back toward their domicile to escape the encroaching rain.

Grish's smile fell, and his face hardened unexpectedly as he fell into step beside Borth. "You have said this to me many times. Some days I think that you mean it, but then I know it is the pain speaking, not my uthak brother. I will not abandon you. If you would give the female a chance…"

"I do not want her pity. She would not come to us willingly as we are. You saw the way she looked at us! At me!"

"She did not look at you in any way other than shock at encountering a male she did not expect. The fault is with the agent who didn't divulge all the details of the contract," Grish corrected irritably.

Borth snorted, not convinced. A smart female wouldn't attach herself to a male who was lamed. They did not make it to shelter before the sky opened up and rain poured down in a heavy wash. It soaked through his clothes, though it rolled easily from his scales. Once under the shelter of the roof's overhang, he shook his head, casting droplets everywhere before entering their home.

"What shall we do today with the rains upon us?" Grish asked as he stopped at Borth's side.

He cast him a sidelong, curious look, and Borth's mouth twisted humorlessly. His brother was far too easy to read. The male hoped that they would spend time with the human. If he was still himself, he would have applauded the idea, happy to convince their pretty mate to enjoy their company.

"Do as you like. I will be returning to my room."

"To do what?" Grish asked in surprise.

"To enjoy my peace and silence," he replied woodenly.

He was about to turn down to corridor to find his room when a shout rose up from the central room. He did not think but reacted to the angry shout. Without hesitation, he barreled into the room, his horns lowered, a war bellow resounding from him even as his eyes sought an enemy.

He stilled at the surprised feminine shout, eyes fastening upon the small human standing upon their resting bench, her hands balled loosely at her sides as she gaped at him.

"Where is the threat, female?" he barked.

"What threat?" she asked in bewilderment. She cast one hand toward the viewing screen with an exasperated snarl. "I can't believe the Calystii think these crappy vids are quality… and even worse, I'm totally sucked into it. This guy is a complete ass, and I think his mate—who he's set aside to add another female to their family—is about to jump into an illicit affair with the Lorgor. Very not cool in their culture, from what I understand. But there's definitely smoldering. Lots of smoldering going on! Now the asshole brought in his new bride, still decked out in the traditional clothes and everything, demanding that his first mate welcome her as a sister. What kind of messed up shit is that? At least get her blessing first. He deserves to have his face rearranged!"

Borth blinked at the female, slowly absorbing the barrage of information torpedoing at him. In her agitation, her face was flushed and her eyes over bright as she cursed and made crude gestures to the viewing screen.

"You are speaking of vids?"

Confusion furrowed her brow, and she cocked her head at him. "Of course."

"I was certain that you were in danger," he bit out.

Realization dawned at that moment, her lips parting before turning up in a wan smile. "I guess I could see how that might be a little alarming."

"A little," he growled.

"Look, it's not that I normally indulge in this kind of thing, but there's really *nothing* to do around here. Though now that I'm into it, I can't promise I can just quit watching. I think the Lorgor is going to steal her away, and I can't miss that."

"I see," he muttered. "I am going to my room."

"You're done in the fields already?" she asked in surprise. "Wow, the workdays around here are short."

"No, a storm has come in. There will be no work today. Just rest."

"I'm pretty proficient in several intergalactic games," she offered.

"No thank you," he grumbled, moving away to a safe distance, far from her enthusiasm. "I would just prefer to rest in the privacy of my room—alone," he added quickly.

Both her eyebrows rose before a wicked grin curled her lips. "I wasn't offering to follow you into your rooms, but now that you mention it…"

Growling, he bent one more glare on his brother before he retreated.

"Where are you going?" she shouted, laughter filling her voice.

He did not care if she laughed. He just needed to get away fast, before he allowed himself to do something dangerous—like have hope. For a moment, he could have imagined that soft smile had genuinely been for him.

CHAPTER 5

"**W**ell, guess it's just us," Crystal said as she turned to the male at her side.

Grish was staring after his brother, grinning in amusement. Shaking his head, his horned crest swinging in the air with movement, he glanced down at her warmly.

"Do not worry, little *katna*. Borth will come around in time. This weather delays our harvest a little, and he worries."

As if emphasizing his statement, a crack of lightning lit up the sky, flashing in the common room as a louder, more ominous sound of thunder roared above. On its heels, rain descended in sheets before her eyes as she watched it fall on the other side of the large windows of the common room. The sound of it hitting the ground and the house carried the sound of a tin rattle being shaken wildly. This was no late summer shower. It was a full-on storm.

"Just how long do these storms last?" she murmured nervously, her imagination providing snapshots of memory of dangerous floodwaters that could follow heavy storms.

"A few hours," Grish soothed. "The autumn rains have begun

a little earlier than anticipated, but they are normal for this time of the year. We will keep busy indoors."

"Yeah? Doing what?" she asked skeptically. As far as she had seen, there wasn't much in the house outside of minimal furniture —and it wasn't due to lack of space. In fact, there was plenty of room to be utilized, much of it wasted, emphasizing the quiet emptiness of the place the Terils called home. "As fun as vids are, I'm used to having more to do to keep me engaged and occupied."

Grish frowned. "This I did not consider. What are things that could make you more comfortable?"

"Well… outside the intergalactic linkup, music would be a good start. And access to the intergalactic media database. I wouldn't mind picking up some educational reading material."

His eyebrows rose slowly. "And you would find that entertaining?"

Crystal grinned up at him. He had no idea. "Dry educational texts are my bread and butter."

His brow furrowed before his expression turned understanding. "Ah, a metaphor. It is basic, regular sustenance for your mind."

"I like to be well-informed," she said with a smile. "It's good to know about where you are and who you're dealing with."

Grish nodded in agreement. "Good. Then we will take a small tour of the house and I will explain some things about our settlement here. It is wise to know friends and enemies."

She looked up at him, an eyebrow arching as she followed him out of the room. "Do I have to worry much about the latter?"

He chuckled and slowed his pace so that she fell into step beside him. "From the other farmers and residents, not so much. Most just wish to be left alone to work their land. The miners are brought in by the Megaraisi Corporation. Most are fine, but the corporation screens more for capability in their mines than for males suitable for our communities. Most do not cause trouble, but our local peacekeepers are vigilant. It's the representatives of the corporation itself that you must watch for. Not the average person employed by them, but those with power and influence on behalf of the company. The Calystii who own and run the Megaraisi Corporation are as ruthless as they come."

Jerking to a stop, Crystal pressed a hand against her heart that lurched within her chest as fear threatened to boil up and drown her. The Calystii were a species with a large population. It was possible that she was overreacting, and they had zero connection to the prince hunting her.

Please let that be the case!

"Calystii, huh?" she mumbled.

Grish nodded. "Their corporation wishes to have every privately owned farm and property under their control. Most settlers are too smart for them, and either avoid or refuse to work under the corporation's authority." His amber eyes gleamed down at her. "It makes the Calystii bureaucrats angry because they wish to own Antari Minor. Our world refuses to give up our freedom for the small comforts they offer in exchange. We will not be owned by anyone. We can't control what they do with their own properties, but we can safeguard our own interests."

Crystal perked up, a small kernel of optimism sparking within her. "They rarely come here then?"

"Here?" Grish snorted and let a deep, rumbling laugh. "They don't try anymore. It has been some time since we have seen one of their representatives on our doorstep."

She let out a breath, a weight falling from her shoulders at that revelation. There would be no Calystii just dropping by and alerting the prince—whichever one he was, since she read that were twelve royal Calystii princes, leaving the identity of her pursuer unknown—of her whereabouts.

"If you are afraid of them, *katna*, Borth and I will keep them away. We will protect you," he said somberly as if reading her mind.

"How did you know…?"

He tapped his wide, flatted nose and smiled. "Teril have very good noses. I do not like smelling fear on my mate. Do not worry. They will get nowhere near you."

Tilting her head, she looked up at him thoughtfully. "They can be persistent… from what I've heard."

His smile widened and he cracked the thick knuckles on one hand. "Then we will… deal… with them."

"It could be dangerous," she replied lightly, despite the lingering tremble of fear as she remembered the violent way they tore up her quarters. It was possible that after the last few years they had forgotten about her and gave up the chase, but she wasn't going to chance it. "You'd really do that for me?"

Grish reached, drawing her against him in a tight hug before releasing her with a chuckle. "Of course. Besides, it is no hardship. We do not like them much anyway."

The forthright statement earned a giggle. It had been a while since she had something to laugh about, and yet twice Grish had drawn it from her. It felt surprisingly good, as had the hug that caught her off guard. Had it been even longer since anyone had shown her any sort of genuine affection?

Her brief ex-mates hadn't hugged her, though she knew some alien cultures didn't show affection the same way as humans, but nor had they seemed inclined to touch her outside of sex. Robby wasn't a hugger, or even much of a cuddler unless he was hogging the bed.

That Grish would hug her was not only unexpected but also threw her off her game. It made her hope for something more, that just maybe she would be safe there, perhaps even eventually loved, and not have to run anymore. Wasn't that what she wanted when she fled Earth to an alien husband? Despite all the disappointments, she was hopeful again—and that hope was dangerous, but she couldn't resist reaching for it with both hands.

She was tired of being scared, of running and hiding. Her Teril mates were big, strong, and attractive. She couldn't see anything not to want. Sure, Borth needed some convincing, but she had eight months to work on him. If worse came to worst, she still had her exit plan.

Grish cleared his throat in response to her silence. "I hope I did not offend. I know humans can be particular when it comes to physical expressions. Terils not so much. We enjoy embracing each other and showing our heart's feelings."

Crystal wrapped her arms around one of his thick arms and hugged it against her. "Not at all," she assured him. "In my family, we hugged a lot. It's been a long time since I've had someone hug me. I had forgotten how good it is."

"It is good," he agreed, his expression brightening as he stopped in front of a wall just before the first room. "Come, little mate. In light of all this heart speaking and your fear, it is good to start here with our tour."

"Here?"

With a nod of his head, he pressed his palm against the center of the wall, the area lighting up before he removed his hand. The wall slid open to reveal a small room filled with weapons. Her eyes widened at the various blades, axes, blasters, and laser weapons that covered the walls they hung on.

"This is the armory," he said. "Much of what you see here is due to our love of collecting fine weapons from all over the sectors, but they are maintained and *very* lethal should the occasion arise where they need to be used. If you're ever in a position where you feel unsafe and we aren't present, come here. I will code your access to this room."

He stepped away and allowed the door to slide shut before proceeding down the hallway, leaving Crystal to collect her jaw and hurry after him. Mouth snapping shut, she hastened to his side, looking up at him with a new appreciation.

If everyone needed a hobby, then that was one she definitely approved of.

The rest of the tour was less eventful, but she learned where the storage areas were, including where emergency food and supplies were kept, where Grish and Borth roomed in case there was an emergency—which had her imagination working over-time, conjuring scenarios that might call for waking them—as well as a side exit that took her directly into the orchard at the side of their property. Fruits hung heavy on the branches. It seemed odd to have an exit leading into the orchard without supplies stored anywhere nearby. The large shed was at the back of the house, visible from the kitchen.

"This is the emergency exit," Grish explained. "There is another one through the kitchen, as you are aware. Teril philoso-phy: 'An emergency exit is good. A hidden emergency exit is even better.' Our orchard can be followed all the way to the lumber producers to the left of our property."

"Wow, you guys are prepared for everything," she said, following him back into the house.

"It is good to be prepared," Grish agreed.

"I don't suppose your species has a Boy Scout system?" At his curious look, she grinned. "The Boy Scouts is an organization for boys—umm, young males—to help them gain useful life skills. Their motto is to always be prepared."

"Good motto," he rumbled pleasantly. A frown tugged at the corners of his mouth. "Are you sure that this is something human males from your region do? I seem to recall a few incidents where a good friend was less than adequately prepared."

Crystal snorted with amusement. "No. Only those who want to do it, and whose parents can fork out the costs for dues and uniforms and take them to meets and various activities."

She remembered how much her younger brother had begged to join the Boy Scouts. He was seven, and it was all that he could talk about before she left home. Her *mamá* had frowned as she read over the material, muttering every now and then about the requirements. In the end, she had decided that it wasn't a good idea at that time, but maybe later. Crystal didn't think later ever came.

Grish gave her a sidelong glance. "Steep costs for something to teach young males to grow to be good males. Do they waive these fees, help transport, and give supplies to the younglings who do not have these credits?"

She blinked. "Ah, no. I think I heard that sometimes they have old uniforms that new kids can wear. But that's all I can think of."

He nodded thoughtfully as he concluded the tour in the kitchen, his large bulk settling into one of the sturdy chairs at the table. "So it is class restricted."

She frowned and leaned her hip against the table beside her. "No, of course not. It is open to all boys."

"Clearly not," he chuckled. "I am not judging. In my society, we have programs for young males and females of different back-grounds, though ours are to develop skills for the trade they might enter into as adults. Everyone knows what is expected of them. They know what skills they should possess even if they end up pursuing another life path, which will require them to work twice as hard to learn things they were not taught as younglings. Regardless, it is understood that if a program is not accessible to everyone, no one can complain when others fail to meet those standards."

"I see. And what skills do *you* lack?" she challenged, her arms crossing over her chest. Although he had a good point, she didn't like to think that aliens saw her species as lacking socially. They had their problems, sure, but so did every species.

Rather than go on the defensive, her large mate smiled easily and leaned back in his chair as he also crossed his arms over his chest, his long, massive tail tapping on the floor beside his foot.

"I cannot cook, unless you count spitting wild game over a fire in emergency if we run out of rations. I can mend a tear or patch a hole but can't make even basic clothes. I am a strong fighter, but I am not great at games of strategy. I never would have made it to a high rank, despite the many high merits of my ancestors, because I lack the patience for it. I have no musical or artistic ability at all, nor do I have any knowledge of politics and the running of the state. Borth and I had to teach ourselves the basics of running a business and a farm because, while farming is a common pursuit of retired warriors, with large farms passed down through our families, we usually manage staff who do the actual work," he admitted. "There are a great many things I cannot do, of course, but those are the most obvious in my mind. I am sure Borth, in his current temperament, could give a longer list of my shortcomings."

The last was offered with another deep laugh. Crystal couldn't help but be charmed by his easy, cheerful demeanor. Even talking about his shortcoming, he continued to be open and approachable —damn near jovial about it. Even his eyes danced at her merrily.

"I don't understand how someone like you willingly entered into a family with someone as sour as Borth," she said in disbelief.

She immediately regretted her observation because his smile fell, and a sadness entered his eyes. He regarded her quietly for a minute before he spoke.

"My brother is a good male. He was not always as you see him now. He was always full of laughter and wit. We entered the Fleet together, the same year we decided to form our *uthak*. We fought many battles together and never did he lose his love of everything in life. Every experience was an adventure for him. The wounds he suffered on Agraadax changed him. Forced into early retirement, and in pain with a prosthetic leg that bothers him with the change of seasons, my brother needs something to make him remember that life is a joy again."

"Is that why you sent for a mate?" she asked softly. "You thought a mate would make him happy again."

"I thought maybe a female would bring him some happiness, remind him of the beauty of our lives here rather than the ceaseless work he confines himself to."

"Then you have thought wrong," Borth snarled from the door, startling both of them. The despair that flooded Grish's face made her heart ache for the male just as much as she hurt for Borth as he spun away from the door and stalked back to his room.

Complete dick or not, he had been dealt a shitty hand.

Grish cleared his throat and pushed to his feet. "Come, let us eat. Borth will return later, I believe."

The simple, tasteless meal of the white stew was extra depressing that night as they ate together in silence. Grish tried to lighten the mood with stories, but even she could tell his heart wasn't in it. It was for that reason she retired to her room early and settled onto her bed to turn on the smaller viewing screen on the near wall. It was a poor distraction until she finally fell asleep.

CHAPTER 6

*B*orth tossed and turned in his bed, his mind replaying his brother's words. He hadn't meant to listen in on their conversation. Absorbed in his dark mood, he hadn't been paying attention to much of anything as he headed toward the kitchen, but Grish's voice reached him just as he entered the room, catching his attention. He had immediately come to a stop at the doorway as his brother explained his reasoning for ordering a mate.

Although he knew it was done out of love, he hated how Grish's observations painted him. Now he would be seen as weak and damaged to their female. Even if she was theirs only for a short time, he had his pride. He didn't wish her to see him as less of a male. Less of a warrior. He had spoken truthfully when he said he did not want her pity.

Now he was sure to have it.

Growling, he shifted again, throwing himself onto his back, one arm shoving any extra pillow under his head to provide space for his ganthli. His tail stretched out between his legs, the thick tip twitching restlessly. He wanted to strangle Grish, and he wanted to carry off Crystal to prove to her that he was not a damaged male. He glanced down at his leg dubiously. He had taken the brace off hours ago when they returned to the domicile.

The metal of his leg was made with numerous easily shifting plates. The medics had suggested it. They claimed it would be more reliable for a male his size rather than those made with synth-flesh prosthetic limbs. He couldn't dispute that. Despite his aches and pains when he overtaxed himself, especially in his knees, he rarely had issue with the limb itself. He barely noticed it, outside of the extra weight that he had become accustomed to revolutions ago, unless he overtaxed himself.

What would Crystal think if she saw it? She would probably shrink back from it and look at him with pity.

He could barely look at it himself without cringing. It was cold metal wired and bolted into place with a long moving part that connected to his femur. The medics had advised that he have the rest of the leg removed and that a full prosthetic with metal reinforcements along his pelvis and spine be added to support the additional weight. At his refusal, they cautioned that there was only so long, even with the added support of the brace, that his knee would be able to take the punishment before the joints ceased to function correctly.

Terils were a large species, with bones and joints made to deal with their weight. He hadn't been concerned about his knee holding out. Instead, he had loathed the idea of losing any more of his body. He still was of that mind, even if he couldn't ignore that the pains in his knee were giving him problems earlier in the day. Earlier in the year, he had been optimistic that his leg would hold out longer than the medics had prognosed, but the agony that he suffered after assisting in battle with one of the awepi—the creatures that dwelled within the mountains—had cured him of that delusion.

Since then, he was unable to ignore what was happening. Whether he liked it or not, he was losing a little more of himself every day until eventually he would no longer have full use of the leg. Unbidden, an image came to mind of his entire leg replaced with one of metal. A long, angry hiss escaped him.

What female would want to look upon *that*?

At least as he was now, he could still disguise it. Even lying in bed, he could pretend that he looked normal. Twitching the blanket over his lower legs, he was able to admire the strong columns of his thighs rising above the bedding. Other than some scarring on his right leg from the surgical tech implants, he appeared wholly himself.

Perhaps if their female saw him this way, she would forget pity. She would see only a strong, virile Teril. He could imagine her eyes growing wide, her pupils expanding with desire. She would slide out of the simple stretchy pants and loose shirt she favored. She would walk toward him slowly, pale golden breasts bouncing with her every movement, hips swaying enticingly. All those dark curls that she kept bound in a wild cluster at the back of her head would spill down her back and over her shoulders like a curtain. A flush would spread over her skin as she heated with desire as she climbed over him, her breath on his skin before she settled herself over him.

Groaning, Borth reached down, his hand wrapping around the thick girth of his cock. The wedge-shaped head already gleamed with the first signs of his arousal. Trailing his fingers over the slickness, he stroked its length, the fine ribbing and smooth scales that ran down the top of his sex glistening with it.

His thighs tightened with pleasure as he imagined her sinking down on it, her sex clenching around his phallus. Her sigh of pleasure would make him grip her hips. Even with her on top, he would master her desire. He imagined the way he would rock her against him as he thrust deeply into her. In his mind's eye, her body jerked with his every thrust, her fragile flesh becoming dewy. He heard humans had a very wet sex, eager, strong cunts. Though he had never lain with a human, or even given much thought to it, now his mind was fully occupied imagining just how wet she would be—her sex squelching around him at every thrust, the musky perfume of her desire filling his nose. He wondered what it would smell like, what it would taste like.

A familiar tightening in his back and thighs spurred him on, drawing faster, firmer strokes along his cock as he imaged the way she would moan and cry out his name as she reached her climax. With one hand, he gripped a pillow and drew it over his mouth, his teeth biting deep into the material, ripping it thoroughly as his climax ran through him like liquid fire. His seed erupted, splashing against his belly and over his hand as the pillow absorbed his roar of pleasure. The world whited out around him for just the space of a second, but he didn't miss the scream that followed.

The pure terror in that feminine cry had him jerking upright and clambering from the bed. His seed still dripped from his belly as he rushed out of the room, ignoring the sharp twinge in his knee. It did not matter. Nothing mattered in that moment except getting to Crystal and eliminating whatever threatened her.

Bellowing out a resonating roar, he burst through her door, not even waiting for it to fully slide open at he shouted the emergency override command. He lowered his head, his ganthli making impact, the loud screech of denting metal eclipsing Crystal's screams. Shaking his head to clear it of the mild disorientation, his eyes immediately latched onto the source of the panicked sound. His mouth dropped open at the sight that greeted him.

Their human stood in the corner of the room, her entire body nude as if she had been interrupted in preparing for bed. Though she was in profile to him, he could see the delightful jiggle of her ass as she threw a shoe at the full-grown tantogal stretched out on the bed.

"Is everything well?" Grish demanded, the bulk of his body slamming into Borth from behind as the male pushed into the room. He did not even glance at Borth, his eyes only searching for their female. A choked sound escaped him as he caught sight of the human and the scaled menace terrorizing her. "Matida! How did you get in here?"

The tantogal swung her enormous wedge-shaped head in their direction, the numerous horns on her head cutting through the air. She chirped happily at the sight of them, rising from the bed on powerful legs seconds before she jumped down and made her way over to them. Crystal's eyes followed the tenacious little monster until Matida arrived at Grish's side, leaning into the scratches he delivered all along her horned brow.

"You have a fucking pet dragon," she observed flatly. "Of course you do."

"Matida is a tantogal," Grish explained cheerfully as he continued scratching the spoiled beast. "They are native to our homeworld. We had lent her to a neighbor to deal with their vermin problem. They must have returned her while we were having evening meal. All the doors are coded to open for her because it is nearly impossible to keep out a tantogal if they want to enter a room. It saves us cost in damages. Strange that she went to your room. Usually she would be in my room, or in Borth's room if she wanted to chew on something of his." He looked at her speculatively, a pleased smile spreading across his face. "She must like you."

"Or she is a menace as I have always said," Borth drawled as he leaned against the damaged door to relieve the weight on his knee. The door protested, but he didn't care. The damned thing was already damaged beyond saving. They would need to replace it regardless. Both pairs of eyes turned to him and immediately widened in surprise.

"Brother, why are you naked?" Grish asked, his head tilting curiously.

"And you, ah… have something on you," Crystal added, gesturing to her abdomen as her face reddened. That did not, however, stop her eyes from roaming over him with an expression of unmistakable appreciation.

That was until her eyes fell upon his leg.

The fantasy he had enjoyed just moments earlier crumbled as her face paled, and his hands tightened to fists at his side. He had been fooling himself. She wouldn't see him as a desirable male. Especially not after seeing him fully naked, dripping with his own spend.

With a low snarl, he turned away, stalking back into the corridor.

"Borth…" Grish began helplessly as he stepped forward.

Ignoring him, Borth pushed his way by, his jaw set with determination.

"Borth, wait!" Crystal called, stopping him just outside of her door. His heart sank, dreading to hear what she had to say. He could not take any more shame. He refused to turn and meet her eye. Silence stretched between them as she waited until, finally, she sighed. "I'm sorry. I didn't mean to embarrass…"

"You did not," he barked sharply. "Is that all you wish to say?"

It was rude, but he just needed to get away. Return to his room where he could attempt to forget that this night had ever happened.

"I guess," she mumbled. "Just… thank you."

"She would not have hurt you," he replied sourly.

"Yeah, but I didn't know that. And you didn't know what was happening when you rushed in to help me. I really appreciate it."

"It is nothing. Now excuse me," he grunted as he made his escape.

He just barely heard her soft reply as he ducked into his room.

"It meant something to me."

Allowing his door to slide shut behind him, he leaned back against it and closed his eyes. He just needed to avoid her until she left. *In eight months.* He groaned, burying his face in his hand. It was impossible.

CHAPTER 7

Crystal stared out the large common room window, rocking back and forth on her heels, and she sang along with the chorus of "Down with the Sickness" brought to her courtesy of the small intergalactic media ear transponders that Grish had gifted her that morning. There was only so much time she could spend watching the vids before she started feeling like a potato pancake. Unfortunately, that distracted her into thinking about food again. Immediately, the song swung into the chorus once more, the heavy beat of the music grabbing her attention, pulling her back into its high energy web.

Had to love Disturbed.

Four days. Four days of the same monotony. Grish was attentive and sweet in the evenings when the males came in from the fields, regaling her during mealtime with stories from their service among the Intergalactic Fleet. It was always a welcome respite, but the rest of the day played out just the same. The same exact replicated food, the same routines. The same unchanging silent treatment from Borth whenever he failed to stealthily avoid her.

She had sort of established a routine with it. Get up. Go to the kitchen. Watch Borth make a break for it. Make small talk with Grish. Eat. Watch her shows until she got bored with the vids. Proceed to spend hours staring out the common room window while attempting to think of some way to amuse herself.

Matida yawned from where she was curled up on a pillow on the floor, showing off two rows of long, sharp teeth, clearly letting her know her opinion on Crystal's effort to self-entertain. Or her taste in music. It could be either—or both.

She had to hand it to the scaly beast. Maybe napping wasn't a bad way of killing a few hours. No doubt Matida would be up for snuggling in bed. Although Crystal had surrendered one of her large pillows for the animal, it ended up doing nothing at all to keep the beast out of her bed. Not that it was all bad.

Matida may have looked like a giant reptile, but her body temperature was higher than Crystal's, and her scales almost silky in texture, despite Grish's assurances that they were extremely resilient against damage, making her a pleasant bed companion. She woke up nearly every morning with Matida's head draped over the back of her neck, a rumbling, purring snore echoing from the beast.

That had been alarming. The first morning, she nearly shouted the house down again in surprise. Not wanting another embarrassing repeat of the guys rushing to her aide, she had managed to restrain it beyond a startled squeak. It had taken a couple of days to get used to the idea of a small wingless dragon for a pet, yet the tantogal won her over.

Really, Crystal had to admit it was the most badass pet a person could have. And the animal's sheer size was reassuring. It made her feel safer while the guys were out in the fields—even if the tantogal wasn't the most entertaining. She didn't play fetch—oh, she might chase something down but always carried it off and hid to chew on it somewhere in private—and really wasn't keen on walks or other activities Crystal might have done with a dog of that size.

Oh well. At least she had access to music now. The real window was also a plus.

Singing along with the lyrics, she watched a fluffy cloud drift overhead. She could see gray clouds in the distance, threatening the possibility of rain sometime during the night, but for now the sun was shining down warmly.

A small flock of ithlek flew past, the strange birdlike animal distinguished by its long, narrow beak, an even longer tongue that helped it scoop up the nasty, biting linsek beetles after spearing them, and a wild fanfare of large crayon-yellow plumage. Several landed in the yard just outside the window, the plumes on their head making them resemble little Victorian ladies nodding to each other as the birds pecked the ground, searching for prey. That each bird's head easily reached her shoulder only reinforced that image. Crystal watched the ithlek hopping in the grass with complete fascination as her music changed to the next track.

Funny, she never imagined that something so simple would become a luxury to her until she became an alien bride. Some of the males she had been "matched" with may have lived in societies with tech she had never seen before, but it didn't make up for the fact that they lived in enclosed homes with large vid screens that mimicked windows, showing whatever recorded scene played on a loop.

This at least felt real. Boring as fuck—but real.

On the other side of *this* window, however, there were real fields in hues varying from russet to yellow, blue, and green. She could also see a cluster of trees beyond the fields. According to Grish, it was an orchard owned by one of their neighbors. Although few farmers grew lumber, nearly everyone had some sort of small orchard, producing different fruits from those of neighboring plots.

Nearer to the house, aside from the occasional avian visitor, there was little worth seeing. There was some empty space that could have easily been made into an attractive garden bed with a little effort. She wondered if the guys would give her a few credits for seeds or starts. Although Grish seemed happy to provide everything she asked for, she did feel a little weird asking for something that really wasn't necessary—especially when she didn't know if she would be staying. But puttering about her *abuela*'s garden, thick with the scent of blooming jasmine that Danitza Alfaro favored, was her most cherished memory.

Staring at the empty beds, Crystal's lips twitched wistfully. Her *abuela* had loved her gardens, but everyone knew that her pride was the prize-winning orchids she patiently grew in her small greenhouse. Crystal hadn't gardened in years, not since she accidentally killed her beautiful orchid, the single plant with its delicate orange blooms that she had been allowed to take home after her *abuela* died. She lost the heart for it, and with all of her time working odd jobs—some of them legit, others toeing the line of black hat territory—and spending countless hours linked in to various systems, she hadn't thought of it in years.

Yet looking at the empty space brought it all back.

She blinked away the memories and looked away. The idea of turning the earth and hoping for something beautiful to bloom like it might have under Danitza's hand was more tempting than she would have imagined. She longed for that familiarity, but it was a big step to take.

Looking out across the lavender grassy stretch of land ahead, she watched the play of sunlight among the pale leaves of the trees that randomly dotted the landscape. There was something soothing about watching the leaves shift with the wind, their color rippling in hues as limbs bent and a brightly clad individual darted behind a tree.

Wait, what?

Squinting, Crystal leaned forward, peering through the pane of what was presumably a kind of alien glass. The red blob moved again, shifting around the side of the tree. A pale gray face framed by scarlet hair so red that it nearly matched the dress itself peeked out in the direction of the house.

Well. That was different.

Touching a finger to small switch nestled at the back of her ear, Crystal deactivated the transponder and turned away from the window. It took her less than three minutes to make it to the front door, and only another minute for her access to the front porch. A crisp autumn breeze whipped around her, and Crystal pulled the fuzzy blanket she had been cocooned in all morning tighter around her as she raised a hand. The female spying on her froze in abject terror.

Had she never seen a human before?

"Hello!" Crystal shouted across the short distance. "It's a bit chilly today. I imagine it's pretty uncomfortable for sitting behind trees." She paused, holding back a laugh as the female glanced around uncertainly, trying to determine who was being spoken to. "Yes, you… behind my tree. Come on in. If you want to, that is."

A startled squeak rang out, and the female turned and bolted away in a flurry of red skirts and hair. Crystal frowned until she felt Matida pressing against her leg and hip. Looking down, she scowled without heat at the large reptile.

"We really need to work on your timing, Matida."

The tantogal rumbled happily and nuzzled her with a playful butt of the head.

"Yeah, yeah, I like you too, you big brat. At least give someone the chance to stick around long enough for your presence to grow on them. Visitors of the non-Calystii sort would be nice on occasion."

Matida chirped, her jaws snapping happily.

"How about a snack, brat? I think I could use a little something. I can try again to fry up some gilig root. I think I almost got a french fry last time."

The animal snorted and let out a sneeze.

"Oh, come on, it wasn't that bad," she laughed.

CHAPTER 8

"Did I see the Wanit female fleeing from our property?" Grish inquired with a curious glance at his mate as he stepped into the domicile.

"Wanit? I don't know. I saw a female. Gray… A lot of red. I couldn't say for sure what exactly she was," Crystal replied as she sat the datapad aside and walked over to help him tug off the sodden leather protective wear wrapped snuggly around his frame. "She sure took off when I invited her in. You would think I was offering to feed her to Matida the way she reacted."

Grish chuckled as the enormous coat peeled off him. "That would be her. The Wanit are a shy species. Not many leave their homeworld. Her family owns the orchard nearest to us. Came with her mate a few revolutions before Borth and I arrived. They're good people, but easily frightened."

Her eyebrows rose, and she regarded him with surprise, seemingly not even noting the way she staggered beneath the weight of the coat as it pulled free. "And nothing has eaten them yet?"

"Like many species, they do have their defenses. The Wanit spit venom. A fine deterrent," he explained.

"I'll say," she murmured as she heaved the jacket over and hung it to dry while he worked his boots off. Turning to him, she regarded the large puddles forming under him with amusement. "Think you brought in enough water with you?"

"Enough. Fitting for the light rain," he agreed.

"You call that downpour a light rain?" She shook her head in disbelief. "Why didn't you guys come inside sooner, like last time?"

He shrugged as he kicked his boots free. "We wanted to get that section of the field done. We made good time and finished before everything became too wet to work. It was worth getting a little wet," he concluded with a grin.

She snorted at him, her eyes darting up as Borth stomped into the doorway. Her mirth instantly dried up, and Grish was sorry to see it go, but not sorry to see the determined, speculative look come to his mate's eyes. She immediately moved to Borth's side. Ignoring his unpleasant growl, she grabbed his coat and began to work it off him with persistent yet gentle tugs.

Grish did not understand his brother's surly behavior. The coats, though sturdy and protective while working in the field, were near impossible to peel off without assistance when they became wet. She was even present when they helped each other that first day. Why was he behaving that way?

"I do not need help," the male snapped, jerking away from her.

Grish drew in a breath, watching for Crystal's reaction. If his brother made her cry, he would pummel him.

Her cheeks reddened, eyes narrowing for a fraction of a moment. In the next, it was gone. She shrugged and released his coat abruptly so that the sodden sleeve slapped Borth with a loud wet sound.

"Suit yourself," she said as she stepped away. She returned to the common room, picked up the datapad, and flopped belly-down on the couch. Matida chirped and tried to jump up with her, but Crystal pushed her back with a laugh. "Don't even think of it, brat."

Grish smiled and pushed himself up to his feet. When he began to head toward his mate to create a little mischief of his own, Borth gave him a disgusted look and put an arm out in his path.

"Are you going to assist me or not?"

Raising a brow ridge, he regarded his brother firmly. "Seems to me you didn't need any help. Did you not say so?"

His brother's glower did not bother him. If he was going to make such pronouncements to their female, then he could deal with the consequences. Borth refused to reply and so Grish strode by, content to spend some time in the more pleasant company of their mate.

"Wait."

Grish stopped and looked at his brother expectantly. The sour expression on his brother's face made him want to laugh, but he held back.

Borth darted a furtive look at Crystal.

Grish didn't even need to look to know that their female was already absorbed once more in her reading. Even after a few days in her company, he was already learning her regular tendencies. He was not surprised, therefore, when the male gestured for him to approach closer.

Dropping his voice, Borth rasped, "I do not want *her* help. I do not want to further shame myself."

"And you think your behavior is not doing that adequately?" Grish replied, his lips twisting with amusement.

His brother's glower deepened, and he huffed in irritation. "Better than a female fawning over a male as if he is helpless. I do not want a female who latches onto me because she feels pity for me," he hissed. "The only reason she has to touch me is out of pity and so I do not want her touch at all. I want to keep my distance from her. I am asking for you to respect that."

Grish sighed and nodded reluctantly. As per his brother's original request, Grish had handled everything that Crystal needed. It was only right since he was the one responsible for being her there. If Borth needed this, he couldn't refuse. He did not like it, but he couldn't force Borth into a mating he did not want. His only hope was that gradually his brother would come to feel some affection toward their female that could plant the seeds of deeper attachment. Crystal had bought them time with her fib.

He prayed that it would be enough.

The lie was clever, and he did not hold it against their mate. Sometimes, on the battlefield, a warrior had to use whatever resources he had at hand in order to win. She had given them eight months. It hardly seemed adequate in light of his brother's stubbornness, but it would have to do.

As he tugged Borth's wet coat off him, he wondered if the female suspected that he knew of her lie. He was no fool, and he knew that she was smart enough not to take him for one. Thankfully, Borth hadn't read the contract and so did not know that there was no such time stipulation within it. Otherwise, Crystal would have been on the first transport off the planet and there would have been little that Grish could have reasonably done to prevent it.

Their little mate was clever.

And practical.

He admired both of those qualities. Over the revolutions they had been farming on Antari Minor, he had the opportunity to see many ordered mates arrive at the outpost. Most of them had been overdressed in what he imagined were strange ceremonial mating gowns. An odd choice on their part as far as he was concerned, but it emphasized how delicate they appeared to be, unsuited for life on the planet.

He almost changed his mind about wanting to order a bride more than once. He had been relieved to see his mate waiting for him in the teahouse in her simple, comfortable dress, drinking intimbar. He had been concerned initially over her lack of belongings but dismissed it quickly. It was an expedient way to travel, and that too was practical.

"Go," Borth grunted as he hung the heavy coat to dry. "You are not looking at her, but I see where your mind is at and it is not here. No need to linger at my side."

Grish grinned at his brother. "She *is* more attractive to look at." He paused when he got no response. "You do agree our mate is very appealing… do you not?"

A grunt was all he received in reply.

"Are you really going to try and tell me that you have not noticed?" he needled.

Borth snorted, his lips tightening. "I noticed. I am not dead." A hard look crossed his face as he kicked his boots off and placed them in the storage unit with the coats. "But she is not our mate. Do not forget, brother: it takes both of us to agree, and I still do not want a mate."

Stubborn male. Grish hoped that Crystal possessed the fortitude to deal with him. He smiled amicably at his brother and shrugged.

"Sure, sure. But there is no harm in enjoying it."

Reddish eyes narrowed on him suspiciously, but after a moment, Borth shrugged. "You can do as you like. I will be enjoying intimbar."

"Perhaps three cups?" Grish suggested. "We rarely use the cooking unit. It would be a shame to start it up to brew from our supply of intimbar grounds without making plenty for everyone. You can surely keep your distance while enjoying a cup of intimbar like civilized people. You can even sit on the other side of the table, if it makes you feel better. I will personally make sure that she is thoroughly occupied."

Borth's brow ridges slammed down, and the four thin nostrils on his flat, rounded nose flared with incense. "I am sure you will. Your *sacrifice* shall be noted and sung of for revolutions to come," he snapped, turning his back to him as he stormed away.

"Does that mean you are making the intimbar?" Grish called out.

The snarl that returned as his brother disappeared from the room was all the answer he needed. Laughter erupted from him. He did not like to see his brother in pain, but the male needed a push to rejoin the living. He had been patient, waiting for his brother to come around since they arrived on Antari Minor, but now was time for action if he didn't want to see Borth sink further into despair every season.

"Did you say something about intimbar?" Crystal asked, her voice a welcome distraction from his train of thoughts.

She had sat up, soft wisps of curls falling loose around her face. At some point in the last few minutes, they had escaped the tight confines of the band containing her hair. She looked rumpled and charming.

He inclined his head and reached out a hand to pull her gently to her feet.

"You did. Borth is preparing it for us as we speak. It is good to warm the blood after the work today."

Her regard turned skeptical. "Borth is… Really?"

"Yes, even my brother has decided he can be civil enough to sit and enjoy a cup of intimbar with us."

"Big shocker there. Seems to me he's more inclined to flee at the sight of me than sit down and enjoy a drink together."

"Ah, so you have noticed that," he replied with a chuckle. "It is his way of protecting himself. If he stays away, there is less chance of becoming attached. A reasonable plan for a stubborn male."

"I see," she murmured, her lips pinching together thoughtfully.

Grish struggled not to grin triumphantly. His female was now armed—and judging by the light gleaming in her eyes, she was plotting something. The human male he had fought beside for so many revolutions would get a similar look when he was plotting another lunatic idea. He was almost eager to see what his little *katna* was thinking. And he had said nothing that could be considered betraying his brother's confidence.

It was, as the humans would say, a win-win situation.

"Come. I am certain that Borth has the intimbar ready by now," he said cheerfully as he placed a hand at the small of her back, ushering her along at his side.

Crystal gave him an amused look but did not object to being herded into the kitchen.

Borth looked over and frowned at their arrival but trudged, albeit reluctantly, to the table where he set down three large steaming cups of intimbar. As they seated themselves at the table, Borth sat as far away from them as he could. The male reluctantly pushed their cups toward them before falling into a stony silence as he stared into his cup.

Grish restrained an impatient sigh. This wasn't quite what he had in mind. Everyone was drinking from their cup, but in complete silence. No one attempted to speak. He fidgeted, trying to think of some way to stir conversation. To his relief, Crystal beat him to it.

Seated close at his side, Crystal made a small sound in her throat and directed a smile at Borth. "Thank you. This is really good."

Borth's eyes glowed with a flash of pleasure as he regarded her over the rim of his cup. He grunted, took a long drink and swallowed. "You are fortunate to drink my intimbar. Grish would have poisoned us with his heavy-handed way around a cooking unit."

"You can cook?" she asked, the delicate eyebrows that graced her face winging upward.

His brother grimaced. "No, but I can make intimbar."

"Ah, well, that explains the reliance on the replicators," she replied, her smile widening. "I suppose one of us will need to learn to cook so we have some variety in our diet."

Borth's expression darkened slightly. "No need. The replicator supplies for all our nutritional needs, even yours once I input your species into its data systems."

"Oh, but at least it'll be a way for me to contribute. I don't mind learning. I mean, I was never anything beyond passable at cooking on Earth, but I'm pretty sure I can guarantee that I won't poison us… I think."

Grish suppressed a groan as his brother's expression completely shut down. The male tipped his head back, draining his cup before pushing up to his feet. He paused only long enough to give Crystal a hard look.

"There is no reason to go through the trouble. You will not be here long enough to make it worth the effort," he said sharply.

Crystal turned in her seat, obviously watching his brother as he stalked to the sanitary unit and placed his cup within it.

"It is no trouble!" she called after him. "Idle hands make all sorts of mischief from what I've heard." A cunning grin lit her face. "If it's not cooking, then it'll be something else. And all it would cost is your company twice a day."

Borth's spine visibly stiffened. "Then find some other mischief," he barked without a backward glance.

With a soft hum, Crystal turned once more to the table and picked up her cup. Grish noted the gleam in his mate's eyes as he met her gaze over its rim. He raised a brow ridge, and her eyes crinkled slightly in amusement.

"Do I wish to know what you have planned?"

"I have no idea what you're talking about," she said, a soft chuckle escaping her.

Grish eyed his mate and took a long drink. She was definitely going to do something. He wasn't able to decipher any meaning from her side of the exchange with Borth. He debated on whether he should warn Borth as they sat in companionable silence with their drinks. Once the last of the intimbar was drunk, he stood, took their cups, and carried them over to the sanitation unit.

As he initialized the sanitation cycle, he heard light steps behind him. Turning, he met her eyes, his gaze tracking her as she leaned forward into his chest. The warm scent of her filled his nose as her soft breasts brushed against him. She wrapped her arms around him and hugged him.

Drawing back, he smiled down at her, his hand lifting to brush through the soft wisps of hair framing her face. He contented himself with that simple touch, though he yearned to draw her closer, to fully press her body against his. The desire to feel her heat and scent her skin crawled through him restlessly.

"What was that for, *katna*?"

"I just… I wanted to show you how much I appreciate you. You're so kind and make me feel safe and wanted." She sighed, her cheek leaning into his touch as if she were positively touch-starved.

One corner of her mouth quirked up. He almost mistook it for amusement until he saw the vulnerability in her eyes. Whereas the first might have made him consider drawing away if he thought she was only playing games, the latter made him want to shield her and claim her as his mate in truth. He rumbled as he placed his other hand on her hip, the curve practically swallowed beneath his grip as he pulled her against him, luxuriating in her closeness as he breathed her in.

Her scent and the feeling of her body against his did something to him, sending heat rushing through his blood. He growled low in his throat and instinctively held her tighter. She stiffened but soon melted against him before he had a chance to loosen his grip. He was aware of every dip of her body, the softness of her belly gently nudging his cock as it began to stir. A tightness at its base made his breath shudder out of him, his hand slipping around to press against her bottom.

At the press of his hardening cock against her, a breathy sound eked out from between those beautiful lips as the smell of her desire bloomed rich and full. Despite the heat of her sexual need for him that began to tune his body to hers, slowly beginning the process of binding them together, it was her need for his strength, support, and devotion that bound him more to her within his heart.

"Of course I want you, *katna*. At this moment, I want nothing more than to show you how much I want and need you," he rasped, his breath fanning her face, stirring the small curls as he leaned forward to draw in the scent of her silky skin. "More than just desire of flesh, I want all of you forever. You have only been here for days and have already brought great happiness into my life."

She pressed into him, a soft groan leaving her, her body soft and welcoming. Her cheek burrowed against him in a sign of stirring affection, but she issued no invitation.

He understood. It was too soon yet.

He leaned down and brushed his lips against the corner of her mouth before he pulled away from her. "I am a patient male, *katna*. I will look forward to the day you welcome me into your bed and your heart. And though he may not admit it, Borth needs you just as much as I."

A delicate shiver raced through her as he set her away from him. It was the hardest thing he ever had to do. He would be patient. There was much pleasure and joy to be had just waiting for them.

CHAPTER 9

$\mathcal{M}$aybe she exaggerated her cooking skills. Her *mamá* had tried to teach her to cook, and there were a few dishes she could make reasonably well that didn't require a lot of effort, but Crystal never had the patience to really develop that particular skill. Especially not after adulthood, when meals were comprised of whatever she could scarf down between work sessions. For the first year on her own, she nearly lived on toaster strudels.

It was sad, but desperate times called for desperate measures.

And not only because she was hoping that Borth would admit defeat, or at least warm up to her a little if she actually went through the trouble to provide him with a decent meal, but she couldn't take another day of the shit the replicator shot out.

That was why she was leaning against the counter, her datapad in hand as she hacked into the programming. It was surprisingly straightforward. Unfortunately, she learned that replicators worked using prefilled materials that could be used to make certain foods. Most standard replicators came with very little stock, and on outlying planets like Antari Minor—cue the suspenseful music—getting anything more varied than the basics was nigh impossible. Still, she wasn't above working some magic and attempting to program the instructions and food profile for a few meals she enjoyed.

Attempting being the key word.

"Okay, let's see how this works," she muttered.

Unplugging the datapad, she set it aside, scooted back in front of the replicator, and made her selection. Vaca frita with french fries. A nice, simple comfort food from her childhood. Setting a plate beneath the replicator, she closed the compartment and waited expectantly as the machine whirred as it initiated into the first sequence. She was hopeful as the box filled with a muted light until it receded, and she got her first look at the food.

Somehow it looked even worse than the crap she was trying to improve upon.

The stringy meat and vegetables gooped on the plate were pale gray. The french fries were perfectly rectangular straws, white as raw uncooked potatoes.

Well, looks weren't everything.

The containment compartment lifted away, and she grabbed the plate of food. Bringing it up close to her face, she took one sniff and gagged. The spices were so far off that it was like sticking her head over hot garbage. The combination she had clearly failed at describing left a base sourness that was just barely covered with the scent of a spice so hot that it stung her nose to sniff at it.

Holding it away from her, she sighed. Tweaking the replicator was out until they got the intergalactic comm system that would allow her to search for replicator codes from Earth resources. Downloading a book or music from an intergalactic vendor on her datapad or ear transponders was one thing, but digging into Earth's manufacturer copyrights to fetch program codes for their replicator needed more juice than she could get with on her little datapad.

Crystal moved to set the plate on the counter when suddenly the ground beneath her feet trembled, then pitched with enough strength to send her crashing to the floor. The sound of the plate cracking was minor compared the rattle of everything surrounding her as she scrambled away from the counters to slip under the table.

Wrapping her arms around the table legs, she ignored the wet mess slicking the front of her shirt and leggings as she ducked her head down and rode out the earthquake. The loud crash of dishes and housewares as they hit the floor filled the air around her. Something struck the table with a bang that made her flinch. Instinctively, she wanted to crawl out from beneath the table, but she forced herself to stay put, reminding herself that it was the safest place in the kitchen.

When at last the tremors subsided, Crystal slowly crawled out, scattered shards of broken dishes biting into her palms everywhere she set her hands down. She hissed with pain, thankful when at last she was able to push up onto her feet. Gripping the side of the table with one bloodied hand, she looked around at the destruction in awe. One short earthquake had demolished so much.

Where the fuck had that earthquake even come from?

She tiptoed through the mess, stopping occasionally to pick up something that had managed to not break when it fell. All the dishes were toast except for one cup, although many other items seemed to have survived well enough. She set her armload and that one lonesome cup down and leaned wearily against the counter. Turning so that her back rested against the edge, her eyes skimmed the room taking in damage.

The door leading out to the rear fields opened as two Terils forced their way through, their wide eyes skimmed over the room anxiously until they came to rest on her. They pushed their way forward, their boots crunching noisily as they rushed over to her. Dark mud streaked across their faces, coats, and arms from doubtlessly being thrown to the ground by the tremors. Borth even had some broken bits of plants clinging to him that he didn't appear to notice as he made quick work of inspecting her.

"*Katna*, have you been harmed?" Grish asked, his voice laced thickly with concern.

"Scared the shit out of me, but I'm fine."

"Not so fine. You have injured yourself," Borth ground out, one of his large hands closing around her left wrist, holding her hand still as he inspected the flesh of one palm and then other.

She grimaced at the mess, her hands stinging. They didn't look that great.

"Yeah, the broken dishes made the floor around the table where I was hiding into a bit of a landmine. It was difficult to avoid them when I was coming out."

"You should have waited. We would have removed the table from above you," Borth chastised. "Stay here."

With a muttered oath, he dug through one of the half-open drawers until he found a strip of cloth. The moment he had it in his hand, he tore it in half and returned to her side. She tried not to wince as he wrapped each of her hands, but it was beginning to really hurt like a bitch as she came down from the endorphin rush. All the while, Grish's large hand stroked her hair and back comfortingly as he murmured softly to her.

Borth snorted at his brother's ministrations, his own face creased with a fierce scowl. Muttering under his breath, he dropped her hands and began to thoroughly inspect the rest of her. It was almost sweet the way he glared at every scratch as if they were a personal affront against him. What was less than sweet was her body's response to his touch as a slow fire kindled within her that grew with arousal at every light touch. Her skin tingled with awareness with every pass.

She needed to get ahold of herself. It was starting to feel a little too good, and she was still focused enough to know that it really wasn't the time for her to body greenlight the idea of getting wild with the brothers.

"I'm okay, guys… Really," she assured them as she gently pulled away from their attentive exploration.

Borth's expression went blank, but then his eyes focused on the slop smeared all over her front. His head tilted as he inspected the gray globs.

"What is that?"

Crystal grimaced down at herself. "That would've been dinner if I'd been successful at reprogramming the replicator."

"But why are you wearing it?"

She shrugged and gave him a crooked smile. "The gods have a sense of humor and decided to send an earthquake the moment I was mourning over my culinary failure. If you still want to try it, feel free to lick it off me."

She batted her eyes playfully, enjoying the way one hand rubbed the back of his neck as if he couldn't decide exactly how to respond. She was mostly kidding—poking the bear, since he was so determined to avoid her—but the other half of her was curious if the sparks would fly the way they had in Grish's arms.

For some reason, she suspected that Borth would be a force to be reckoned with. His eyes ran over her possessively, desire flaring in his eyes at the suggestion as his gaze fastened on the way the damp shirt clung to her curves. He swallowed, but eventually shook his head.

"Lick it off… No. It smells like something Matida killed and regurgitated," he muttered with a wrinkle of his flat nose. Obviously, he wasn't going to pull his punches about how he *really* felt about her attempt at improving their meal experience. He expression morphed into a glare as he stared at the replicator. "After we clean up this mess, I will check the replicator to make sure you did not delete what edible food we have available."

"Edible is debatable," she replied—perhaps a little louder than she intended.

His dark look transferred to her, but he didn't reply. Instead, he made his way over to a narrow utility closet where he pulled out something that resembled a broom. Crystal was surprised to see something so low-tech in the efficient household.

"You aren't going to summon a cleaning droid or something?"

He snorted and shook his head, but lapsed back into silence, leaving Grish to reply. Obviously Borth's social hour had timed out for the day. He was back to ignoring her as he set to work with the broom, sweeping up a large pile of broken dishware. Grish nodded to the shards as he began to stack and re-store the things that had survived the earthquake.

"The droids are good at cleaning up dirt and even your little cooking experiment, but not so good when it comes to larger rubbish. We will make quick work of this and leave the droids to clean the remaining fragments and spills," he explained.

"Ah, okay."

She cleared a small pile of rubble and began to join Grish in his task of separating out and returning undamaged goods to the shelves in the storage units lining the large facing wall. As they worked side by side, Grish turned an amused glance in her direction. Scooting closer, he dropped his voice into a hushed whisper.

"I applaud your attempt, but did you have to do something so dramatic as attempt to destroy the replicator?"

She rolled her eyes. "I wasn't trying to destroy the replicator," she whispered back.

Grish frowned slightly. "I do not think poisoning him would be a way to endear him to you either."

"I wasn't trying to do that either," she hissed. "I honestly thought if I improved on the crap that thing spewed out that maybe it would put him in a better mood."

"You plan on seducing my brother through food?" Grish raised a horned brow ridge in her direction, his look so utterly skeptical that she wondered if she was entirely on the wrong track.

His lips suddenly quirked, and he leaned forward to press a kiss against her lips—too fast for her to even respond. Heated eyes trailed over her as his tongue stroked over his full bottom lip. She leaned forward, her belly warming with excitement, hoping that he would repeat the kiss, but he shrugged good naturedly and drew back, his eyes sparkling with mirth.

"Eh, no harm in trying, *katna*. But maybe go about it in another way."

With a mental groan, Crystal got a hold of her eager libido and strangled it back under control. It was a bad time to entertain the idea of getting freaky with the alien when the house looked like an explosive had been detonated within it. Even if the earthquake hadn't happened, she would still be back to square one. Grish was right; she was going to have to approach the matter from another direction. She wasn't the Martha Stewart of Antari Minor, or even a very basic imitation of one.

Shit, if Martha Stewart were there, she could probably have taken some of those root things that the guys grew for Matida to chew on, worked some clever culinary magic with the slop from the replicator, and turned them into a gourmet meal. No doubt it would have been better than Crystal's attempts to fry the hell out of them in a desperate bid to satisfy her craving for french fries.

Good idea or not, she wasn't going to be able to win over Borth through his stomach. So much for doing things the easy way. She sighed morosely at the thought.

"Yeah, that idea was definitely a bust," she agreed, her eyes fixing on Both's broad back at the other side of the room. He hadn't bothered to look her way even once since his last exchange of words with her. He was determined as hell, that was for sure.

Little did he know that she was stubborn too. It was time to get creative. He couldn't ignore her forever.

CHAPTER 10

Grish frowned at the small stretch of flattened, limp agrim. The thick red stalks that bore clusters of grain fared worse than any of the other crops. It was also the most felt loss. Agrim grain was a staple throughout the Intergalactic Union and brought the highest yield of credits. The crop did not suffer much damage—without a doubt, it could have been much worse—but the losses were still felt. He sighed and swiped a hand down his face.

The agrim still had another week or two to finish maturing while they finished the harvest rotation among the other fields. The damaged grain would have to be cleared out to get anything at all for it, but the best they would get for the slightly immature grain was trading it as livestock feed. If they were fortunate, they might get a few paltry credits for it, but most farmers bartered for supplies instead. Few had the extra credits to expend before the harvest was brought to market.

At least the damage was contained mostly there. The vegetables, beans, and melons they had spent the morning inspecting appeared largely undisturbed. There were a few fallen limbs in the orchard and a few of the weaker trees had toppled, but fortune was with them in that they had harvested the fruits just days earlier.

Borth grunted and kicked at a clump of agrim nearby. "Could have been worse."

Grish nodded. "We will collect the grain and take it with us when we take the saprili fruits to sell at the market. Crystal should enjoy it," he added with a fond smile. "She has been restless. It will be good for her to meet some of the other females in our community."

His brother frowned at him. "Do you think it's wise to expend any more time than necessary at the market? An earthquake is unheard of. This activity reminds me of Fantan City. It seems foolish to linger in town with this new activity, especially to entertain a female who is only here for a short time."

As if to emphasize his point, a light tremor ran beneath their feet. There had been several since the quake yesterday, and each of them made Grish's skin prickle with a nervous energy.

Fantan City had been obliterated when a series of quakes preceded a massive volcanic eruption from the fertile mountainside in their home province. Although they had been young and didn't live close to the city, he still remembered the ash that coated his family's farm. They had complete crop loss that revolution, and it had taken a considerable amount of his family's wealth to restore the farm the next season after that.

The only thing that kept him from worrying excessively about it was that the tremors were light and occurring further apart. There were no further incidents, and it seemed that they were on their way to ceasing altogether. If anything was going to happen at all, it didn't appear to be happening yet. He couldn't say with any certainty if they were dealing with the same sort of problem. It was possible that they were projecting their fears on an unknown situation. It was nothing that he felt inclined to worry their female over by insisting she remain at home.

Besides, he wanted their mate to find things about their world that she enjoyed. He saw how restless she was. He wanted her to feel like she belonged there with them, not like a visitor trapped in their home.

"We will take precautions, but I do not see any reason to worry yet. The tremors are subsiding. Nothing to get excited about… Not yet."

Borth gave him a doubtful look but reluctantly nodded, his lips pressed into a thin line as he looked toward their domicile. "Will you tell her?"

Grish shook his head. "What do *we* tell her? We do not have enough information. I do not wish our female to worry needlessly about something that may never happen. She is already anxious enough now that you are hiding from her."

"I am not hiding. I am reinforcing the separation and avoiding temptation," Borth replied firmly. "I do not see any reason that it should make her anxious."

"I suppose it's natural that you, intended mate or not, keep to the shadows and darkness like a thief at all hours. All to avoid one small female." Grish's lips tipped upward in amusement. "But perhaps she should not take it that personally, yes?"

"And I should not take personally that I cannot figure out what she did to the lights in my room?" Borth shot back. "She is fortunate that I decided on this course of action, because I would have happily wrung her neck for the way she programmed them to go on and off every time I enter the room."

"That sounds very distracting."

"It is more than distracting. It is maddening," Borth gritted out, a dark scowl on his face.

Grish chuckled. "Maybe if you had asked her nicely, she would have fixed it for you, and you would not be suffering from it."

Borth's scowl grew fiercer. "I would rather endure than give that female the pleasure," he snapped. With violent swing of his tail, he spun around and stalked off in a foul mood. It was more entertaining than Grish had anticipated, and he could not resist shouting out after his brother.

"Maybe if you did not fight your attraction as you do, you wouldn't be engaged in a battle of wills with the female!"

Borth did not respond except to shoot a crude human gesture at him as he went to retrieve the separation processor. Grish grinned after him but didn't attempt to cajole his brother into a better mood as they worked silently beside each other.

During the heat of the midday, they stripped off their shirts and the thick leather coats they wore while operating harvester machines. With the amount of work ahead of them, it was obvious that they would not be getting to the machines that day. Chests bared to the warm air, they cut the large clusters of grain free from the stalks and cast them into the machine settled in the space between the rows of grain. They had nearly cleared the entire mess when a voice rose in greeting, attracting their attention from the loose straw they were binding into tight bales.

"Borth, Grish… good day!"

His head turning to the voice, Grish squinted and broke out into a welcoming smile as he spotted the Wanit male striding between the rows. Despite his gray skin, his brilliant red braid and characteristic red cloak clasped around his shoulders were clearly visible among the greenery.

"Nargis, good day. How are you faring, friend?" he called back cheerfully.

Borth raised a hand in silent greeting to their neighbor before returning his attention on his own bale.

"Well enough," the male said, his eyes resting on their work with a little frown. "I see you suffered some loss from the earthquake as well."

"Not too bad," Grish replied. "It was worse in the house, but at least our female was not injured."

Borth let out a noncommittal grunt, but thankfully did not volunteer his opinion. No matter how much he detested the situation, Borth was just as private as Grish and wouldn't contradict him in front of others.

Nargis gave him a confused glance, but the male's expression cleared, and he gave them a relieved smile. "Ah. I heard that you have a strange alien in your home, but I was not aware it was your mate. My Talimia will be relieved to hear that. She had come by to propose a barter but was very concerned when she noted the stranger on your property. She hurried home to tell me in case you needed any help disposing of it, but with the earthquake I completely forgot about it until now. A good thing you were not in any danger," the male chuckled.

"That explains why we saw her fleeing from our home," Grish replied. "She appeared to be in a hurry, and Crystal had no knowledge of why she was running from our property. Be sure to tell your mate that we appreciate her thoughtfulness and not to worry. In fact, she would be welcome to come any time to visit with our female. Crystal gets a little bored and would enjoy the company, I think."

Nargis appeared a bit surprised at the idea, but he regarded him thoughtfully. "Perhaps. Talimia misses her female relations and friends from our home world. Time with another female may be welcome."

"The earthquakes are worrisome. Maybe once things settle down. You don't think that there is something to them, do you? In all the revolutions here, I have never felt even the slightest tremor until now, and even a day later we are still feeling them."

Grish frowned with uncertainty. "Difficult to say what it was, but we will remain cautious."

"If you could keep us informed, we would be indebted,"

Nargis replied quietly, clearly just as disturbed as they were by recent events.

"You said she came to propose a barter. What did you have in mind?" Borth broke in.

The other male immediately perked with the discussion coming around to business. "Talimia has some baked goods and preserved fruits she's been working hard on over the last several rotations. I hope that will make a suitable trade for some help updating our new watering systems. I had them replaced, but the programming is off."

Borth suddenly smiled as he threw the last bale into the transporter cart. "We have just the person for the job."

Although Grish didn't approve of Borth offering their mate's services without consulting her, he could not wait to see the look on her face when the food was brought to the house. He knew that she tired of the fare from the replicator. They didn't care for it themselves and enjoyed such rare treats from their neighbors, but not knowing how to do much with ingredients had prevented them from filling their house with much in the way of foodstuff. He was determined to remedy that when they went to town, but that wouldn't happen for a few rotations yet. There was little doubt she would appreciate the exchange, even if it cost a small amount of labor. He knew she would be better equipped to handle it than either he or his brother blundering their way through basic programming with a datapad until they hit on something close.

He squinted at their own fields as they finally retired for the day, the sun already beginning its descent. Perhaps he should have Crystal look over their own watering and feeding systems from their crops. The auto-start often malfunctioned, and they were forced to manually start the systems.

He turned to ask Borth his opinion only to find that his brother had already disappeared. No doubt the male made use of the door nearest to their own quarters to enter without their female being aware. He wondered how well that was working out for his brother. Clearly, regardless of whether he was near her or not, their female was more than capable of making her presence known. Just how long would Borth hold out?

Not long, he would wager.

Grinning with amusement, Grish entered their domicile in a cheerful mood despite a long day of dealing with the damages to their farm. The kitchen was empty, as to be expected, but it didn't take him long to find their mate sprawled in the common room with Matida, dark curls falling over her face from where they escaped her hairband as she bent over the datapad.

"*Katna*, here you are. Good. How was your day?" he rumbled as he wedged himself onto the high-backed bench behind her.

He dropped his nose into the crook of her neck and breathed in the perfume of her skin. There was a trace scent of the cleansing gel that they used clinging to her, but it did little to cover her delectable scent. His tongue stroked the flesh, and she immediately squirmed back against him, her rump nudging his cock enticingly. A low growl vibrated through him as his hands tightened on her hips, holding her in place. He ground against her, letting her feel the length of his stiffening cock, refusing to let go of her until she giggled and slapped back at him with one hand.

"Hold that thought, handsome," she murmured, smiling as her fingers skimmed over the pad. "Did you know that your house is absolutely amazing to me? We have certain programmed features in our homes on Earth, but literally everything in your house is routed through a central system. It's so high-tech that anyone on Earth would say that your farm is, outside of that replicator, the height of luxury, and very susceptible to manipulation if one knows what they're doing."

He chuckled and nuzzled her, gratified when she leaned back into his touch, welcoming it. "Most would say that the domicile's tech advances make it not only safer, but also more secure from those without access clearance. And more comfortable... Though I'm not so certain of that after I heard what you did with Borth's lights. Very clever."

He didn't say that it was also disturbing how much power she had should she choose to use it against them outside of the harmless prodding at Borth.

She glanced back at him over her shoulder. "Not so impressive when you consider that you did half the work for me by giving me complete access to your home. I'm not so sure I could hack through your security systems. Maybe if I had enough time," she said with a small laugh.

He peered over her shoulder at what appeared to be a schematic of their domicile with various systems highlighted. "What are you doing now?"

A smile played on her lips. "You'll see." She held up a finger. "Wait for it."

An enraged bellow echoed through their home, making the walls shake. Rather than cower, their female chortled gleefully and set aside her datapad. Her hands no longer occupied, she turned in his arms, draped her legs over his thighs, and grinned up at him.

His brow ridges rose as he heard another roar echo. "What did you do?"

"I may have changed his access clearance on his room. Kinda hard to hide in there if he can't get in."

She twitched as a third enraged bellow issued, followed by the sound of a fist hitting metal.

"Don't worry. It won't last long. I put it on a timer, so he should have access..."

The sound of something heavy falling vibrated through the domicile. Grish was certain that he knew what—or more accurately, who—fell.

"Female!" Borth roared enraged.

"Now," she said. She cocked her head, listening, but when Borth didn't storm into the common room, she sighed in disappointment and leaned forward against him, her lips feathering against his bare chest in a brief, playful caress. "I don't think I mentioned how much I like this look," she observed with an appreciative look.

"It is a good look for me," he agreed, provoking laughter from his little female.

"Not one for modesty, are you?" she teased.

He feigned confusion. "What good is modesty when one's desire to please their female is far more important than their vanity? I take pride in being pleasing for my mate."

"Not quite your mate," she corrected, her fingers skimming over the bulge in his pants.

A shiver ran through him, and he drew in a harsh breath at the delicate contact.

"Not quite," he agreed. "But I look forward to the day that I may claim you."

"If Borth agrees," she said with a wan smile.

"If Borth agrees," he confirmed with a light kiss before drawing away from her seductive touch, his fingers roaming at the covered seam of her sex and the swell of her breasts until they were no longer within range of contact.

He immediately missed the intimate contact between their bodies. He was close—so close—to throwing away the promises that he made himself to wait for his brother to be ready to take things to the next step. It was only with great determination that he was able to pull back.

He would not lay with her until his brother was ready.

Her breath escaped her in a ragged sigh, one that he felt down to his bones. Running a hand against her cheek, he kissed the silky skin. He could at least give her one small thing to look forward to.

"Let me tell you of the offer made to me today," he murmured.

The pleasure that bloomed on her face as he told her of Nargis's proposal was almost as sweet as tasting it on her skin. Almost. His lips caressed her again, sipping at the flavor of her with his stroking tongue when she threw her arms around him in excitement.

Borth could not yield soon enough for him.

rystal took another bite of the fruit-filled pastry that had been set in front of her. The fact that Grish was watching every single bite with great interest only enhanced the appeal of the experience as she made a subtle show of sucking the fruit filling from the utensil and licking it clean with relish.

Not that she wouldn't have done that anyway.

It was fabulous, definitely the best pie she had had in quite a while. It was strange to consider that something like pie would be an intergalactic concept, but she supposed there were only so many ways one could make a doughy pocket filled with goodness. The fruit itself was unfamiliar, with a sweetness added that cut through the natural tart flavor. It was like eating a pie made from Granny Smith apples.

As she devoured the last bite, she regarded the female Wanit seated at the other side of the table. It was strange seeing her up close. The gray of her skin was less Area 51 steel gray and more a soft, buffed hue that contrasted with the scarlet braids that fell over her shoulders. She wasn't wearing red this time, though a red cloak had initially covered her pale yellow dress. Despite a simple design, like a long tunic, it was embroidered with so many tiny beads accenting the work that Crystal felt plain sitting next to her. *And* Talimia could cook!

Well, Crystal couldn't hold that against her. She had fed her, even if the female stared at her as if she were afraid that Crystal would jump her and try to eat her as well. Smothering a chuckle, Crystal licked her lips, catching the last traces of flavor with her tongue.

Catching Grish watching her, she winked at her mate, earning a lascivious grin for her effort as she shifted uncomfortably in the chair. It was almost gratifying to see that he enjoyed it as much as she did. Poor Borth was missing out on the food *and* a show. That performance didn't even need any acting on her part. Gods, it was good. If anyone deserved to be awarded the honorary title of Martha Stewart of Antari Minor, it was likely Talimia.

With a longing look at the other goodies laid out on the counters, Crystal put her spoon down with a satisfied sigh before smiling at the other female. Although Talimia was obviously shy, the female's gray skin stained with a purple flush at her obvious pleasure—and likely some of Crystal's food flirting with Grish—as she returned her smile.

"That was wonderful. Thanks, Talimia."

"You are quite welcome," the female replied, a brilliant smile breaking out across her face. "Nargis and I appreciate what you were able to do with our programming, and in so little time, too. This was the least we could do. I am very glad you enjoyed it."

"We enjoyed it very much, didn't we, Grish?" Crystal teased her big mate, to the delight of their guest, who muffled her laughter behind a hand.

He chuckled and nodded in agreement before kissing the top of her head and discreetly clearing the dirty dishes. As much as she loved to tease him, she appreciated that he angled his body so that their guest wouldn't get an eyeful of the large erection straining against his pants. Not only because it would mortify the

Wanit, but because as the days passed, Crystal was feeling increasingly possessive of her males—even Borth, despite his pigheaded avoidance of her.

It really wasn't even because they made an effective barrier against the Calystii. She hadn't given them much thought as of late. No. She genuinely enjoyed being with them, despite being stuck in the middle of nowhere. Even that was starting to look up after meeting the Wanit neighbors. Maybe she would actually be able to do something useful.

It would never be a hopping metropolis, but just how much was she going to miss the lights and parties? It wasn't like there wasn't a town. Besides, linking in was where everything was at, especially with alien tech. Once she was able to link in, it would open worlds up to her, even on a farm. She already knew that Grish had put in an order for the equipment.

Overall, she was starting to feel hopeful.

The only thing that cast a shadow over things was the knowledge that her position was tenuous at best. She wasn't really their mate, and regardless of her presence, she knew that Borth and Grish could still be considered eligible males. It was frightening knowing how fast things could change, though it wasn't something she was about to admit to anyone.

It would help to allay her worries some if Borth started responding to her methods. He was avoiding her, no matter what torment she set up for him. Just that morning, at early hours so that she knew he would not yet be out of his room, she hacked into the comm system in his room to give him a personal wake-up call. Through the comm, she could hear him curse her soundly, but he refused to speak directly to her and, as far as she could tell, ignored the incident completely.

Stubborn male.

Grish leaned down and brushed his nose against her jaw affectionately. She didn't even try to resist melting into his touch. At least he wasn't a difficult nut to crack. He wasn't shy about his interest in her nor about showing affection.

She loved that. He seemed to know exactly when she needed that extra physical contact.

"I am going to step outside and join Borth and Nargis—if you will be all right?" he murmured against her skin.

She wanted to roll her eyes because it wasn't like the Wanit was going to try and murder her. But at the same time, she wanted to crawl into his arms, grateful that he was making sure she was okay when she was feeling a little emotionally vulnerable.

At her nod, she felt his lips pull into a smile before they brushed against her in a feather soft kiss. "Good. I believe that my friend is getting ready to bring out the tansil. We will enjoy a pleasant smoke while you... do female things," he finished uncertainly.

Crystal watched appreciatively as he left the room, then turning finally to fully face the other female. With the Wanit's nice clothing and incredible homemaking skills, Crystal realized she didn't know what to talk about. What could she possibly have in common with her? Generally, she had a hard time making friends with other women, even among humans.

"I guess we're supposed to do female things. Not sure if I know what those are." She laughed uncomfortably. "My skills involve more tech than socialization with other women. In fact, my abilities in the latter and most things my *mamá* would have considered part of a woman's daily life are pretty lacking. I may be able to plug into the systems and do some mean coding, but there's no way I could ever have made all this wonderful food."

There. Might as well go for blunt honesty.

To her relief, the other female didn't appear shocked or dismayed at her admission. Instead, Talimia's smile widened with amusement, her shyness dissipating in the face of Crystal's honesty. The female leaned forward, her dark eyes sparkling.

"My guess is that they expect us to do the exact same thing that they are, except in the comfort of the kitchen rather than walking around in the dirt and mud. The scenery is lovely, but sometimes I am not certain what exactly I am supposed to do any time I go out my own door." She chuckled, her low, throaty voice comforting Crystal. "Wanmira has such spaces, but I was raised in one of the largest cities of our province. Sometimes all of this space is… overwhelming."

Talimia shrugged and pulled out a long, thin silvery pipe tipped with a small bowl. It looked delicate, with beautiful engravings of flowers with small inlaid gems. Crystal would have assumed it must've been for something else if she hadn't watched Talimia place a small, sticky lump in the bowl. Even that she produced from a decorative container that she retrieved from a small, ornately stitched pack on her belt.

"It is the way life is here. I do enjoy the peace of being able to do as I like without fretting over the expectations of my family. They did not approve of Nargis because he was from a lesser family. He grew up doing all of this but came into the city for trades. When I saw him, I knew that he was the one I had to hunt."

Crystal startled. "I'm sorry—did you say you *hunted* him?"

The Wanit grinned, displaying surprisingly sharp—though small—fangs.

"In my culture, the females select the males they wish for as mates and engage in the hunt. We pursue them and demonstrate our interest. Traditionally, this was done with the assistance of one's sisters and closest friends. We track and corner the male so that she can safely pin him and make her proposal. The male runs to prove their strength and ability to provide. It is expected of him, even if he chooses to decline the female. It is considered a great insult to not run at all. My family did not support my choice, and my friends abandoned me because if I mated with him, I would no longer retain my position in our society. But I hunted him all the same, and Nargis gave me a long and difficult pursuit. He is a worthy mate," she finished with a satisfied smile as she brought the pipe to her lips.

Crystal watched in fascination as Talimia pressed a small button on the pipe that made the bowl glow as it heated the sticky substance. The female took a puff on it before allowing a spicy-scented smoke—that reminded her only vaguely of a seasonal mix of clove, ginger, and cardamom—to escape from her mouth in an elegant stream.

"How long was this hunt?"

Talimia licked her bottom lip thoughtfully, fondness burning in her eyes. "Five glorious months. He took me on quite the chase," she answered with a laugh.

"I guess I shouldn't feel so bad that I've been here for a few weeks now and still haven't managed to get Borth to stop running away from me," Crystal muttered under her breath.

Another peal of laughter left her companion, letting her know that her new friend had definitely heard her.

Damn, were all aliens so sharp?

"My Nargis has spoken often of your Borth. Says he has never met a male who so desperately wanted a mate but was terrified of actually acquiring one. He had offered more than once to introduce him to daughters and sisters of business acquaintances, but Borth has always rejected the idea, no matter how much interest he appeared to show. I am glad that Grish found a way to work around it, but now you must hunt your male. It is not easy to hunt alone—I know that much from experience." She sighed as she handed the pipe to Crystal.

Crystal glanced down at the small pipe. "This isn't a narcotic, is it? I'm not really into doing drugs. I tried acid once just before linking in with a virtual reality unit in my youth, and now I prefer to keep my mind under my complete control."

"No, there is no harm. It is a pleasant sensation breathing it in because the smoke is cool and refreshing. It is good for relaxing," Talimia added with a small smile. "But do not feel obligated if you do not wish to partake. Not everyone enjoys spice."

That didn't sound all that bad, though it was hard to link the scent of the spices to anything like what the other female described. Curious, Crystal put the pipe to her lips and pushed the button as she drew in a small amount of fragrant smoke. It was like breathing in the cool spring air after a rain as it filled her lungs. Even her tongue tingled as the smoke passed over it. She smiled and attempted to hand it back, but her friend put up a hand and produced a tiny yellow sphere.

"Wait. Try it this way first. I do not have many of these left, and I will have to make another order to our homeworld, but you must try it with the zanilo. It comes in many different flavors, but this is my favorite. It enhances the flavors and adds a fruity bite. Just place it under your tongue."

Crystal did as instructed, and a small shiver of pleasure ran through her, the fruity, citrusy flavor bursting over her tongue, mingling with smoke as if she were eating the most decadent dessert.

"This is amazing!" she said with surprise and returned the pipe. "I'll bet smoking with another chunk of that pie stuff will be epic."

The female's eyes danced with laughter. "Ah, yes, it's quite good with ombranel, if that is the pie of which you speak. Perhaps we should have a bit more."

As they enjoyed additional slices of ombranel, they continued to pass the pipe back and forth. Crystal had never felt so relaxed without her mind also feeling sluggish and sleepy. Instead, she felt like she had just enjoyed a wonderful sauna. She felt so boneless and comfortable that not even the tiny tremors bothered her. After the last few days, she had almost become accustomed to their daily occurrence. Whatever their source, they didn't seem to be going anywhere and weren't strong enough to be any kind of inconvenience. Most times, she could barely feel them.

Talimia sat back with a content sigh. "So, tell me of your hunt."

Crystal filled her in on everything she had tried, and the female nodded thoughtfully.

"You have done well by making sure you are on his mind every day. I have known some females in solo hunt who have used this strategy with particularly elusive males. I would perhaps remind you that the hunt is as much sensual as it is presence. You want him to be eager for you and yearn for you even though he is running."

"Sensual, huh?" Crystal said around another puff of smoke.

"As for your attempt to appeal to him through food—well, I can help you with that. I will teach you myself. I will send you a complete list of what you will need to acquire from the market so we can begin daily lessons."

Crystal stared, a warm feeling settling within her. "You would do that? Are you sure it won't be an inconvenience?"

"Not at all," Talimia retorted cheerfully. "I am actually looking forward to it. It will be good practice for if Nargis and I manage to produce offspring—Wanit breeding cycles being as infrequent as they are. I do hope to have a daughter to pass all my knowledge on to one day. Until that day, I have you. We can start in a week. It will give me time to prepare a menu of where to start."

A grin stretched over Crystal's lips. "Sounds like an excellent plan."

CHAPTER 12

Crystal hummed over her datapad as it communicated directly with Borth's personal viewing screen in his room. She was due to start her cooking class in two days, and now Grish told her that Borth wasn't going to go with them to the market. She hadn't even fucked with him at all for a couple of days, hoping to see if her sudden absence would bring him out seeking her—out of suspicion if nothing else. It hadn't worked.

This avoidance thing was getting out of control. It had been several days since she last saw him. For such a big guy, his ninja skills would have been laudable if he weren't pissing her off so much. Which brought her to her current act of vengeance.

Or rather, hunting, as Talimia put it.

In fact, with no response from Borth at her latest tactic, she was finally taking her friend's advice. The Wanit had kept in touch almost daily through comms, to see how things were going and to encourage her. She had heartily approved of Crystal's plans. And although it was no worse than any of her other tactics, this one was bound to push in a way that the others had not.

It even pushed *her* out of her own comfort zone. More

comfortable in the digital world than the physical world, she never felt particularly sexy or desirable.

Now she was using it to further her ends with Borth and prayed that it worked.

Despite her awkwardness over what she was about to do, she felt no shame at all over it. She wasn't ashamed of her body and had too much to lose if she didn't win. Sure, she still had her escape plan if all else failed, but that little taste of the way things might be with the Ugaar brothers, they had occupied her thoughts nonstop for weeks now, her imagination growing increasingly erotic.

The kisses she shared with Grish were starting to frustrate her more every day, ramping up her desire and leaving her unfulfilled. Lately, she had begun imagining that Borth was with him and the things the males might do to her if given full rein. That had been a revelation for her as she realized just how much this hunt was affecting her. She already knew that she wanted him, but the erotic fantasies were making her urgency—and Borth's absence— more keenly felt, especially knowing that Grish was holding back, waiting for his brother.

Although she wanted them and wanted to be a part of their family, she wasn't one to lie to herself and insist she was in love with them. She didn't know *what* she felt. She wasn't even sure if it was Grish's thorough wooing and reluctance to move their relationship on to the next level that made Borth more appealing than he might have otherwise been to her. There was also the possibility that she was reading the entire situation wrong and he truly didn't want her. If that was the case though, he was going to have to have an actual full conversation with her and spell that shit out.

Until then... Well, she didn't want to miss out on finding what could possibly be a forever kind of thing. Was it wrong to want at least a taste of what it could be like, of having a family for however long she could, if nothing else?

It may have been masochistic to push the issue because if he truly didn't want her around, this was all going to backfire. She couldn't ignore that possibility. Yet she couldn't resist reaching for it all the same. The fact that he was the biggest, grumpiest male she had ever met didn't dissuade her in the least.

She always did have the problem of wanting to have what she was told that she couldn't.

Borth drew her to him despite the fact that he kept himself isolated with his pain, wearing a big invisible 'fuck off' sign presented to the whole world. She got that and respected it, but she also saw how close he was with Grish, and she wanted that too. For whatever reason, she wanted to be one of the people he desired to keep close, to shelter beneath that big snarly defensive barrier he carried around with him.

She longed for someone to trust and want her that much.

If she were a better person, she might have left him alone and hoped he might change his mind and approach her in his own time. It just so happened that she believed that sometimes one just had to rip off the bandage and move on rather than endlessly licking wounds and wishing for things to be the way they once were.

This was just her version of ripping the bandage off.

She grinned as she entered the last bit of code. He really was a naughty boy who was desperate for someone else's touch, from what she could see from the stream she was interrupting.

He probably wasn't going to appreciate that. Oh well.

If she couldn't stare at him in person, then he would have no peace from her likeness standing in for her. Setting her datapad aside, she lay back, her hands stacked behind her head, and waited.

orth slipped into his sleeping quarters silently, sighing in self-disgust. No matter how much he attempted to avoid the female, he was drawn to her, spying on her without her knowledge. Not even Grish knew how much he lusted after her from afar, how much he wanted her. Her smiles were imprinted on his memory, no less than watching as his brother roused her passions with his kisses and touch.

Borth couldn't keep himself from imagining himself in his brother's place, bringing need to their female. It was something he couldn't have and shouldn't want as badly as he did. He shouldn't stalk her from the shadows, watching her work as she came up with one devious plan after another to torment him… but he did.

In truth, he felt foolish working so hard to evade the presence of one small female who for all appearances seemed intent on having him, but part of him did not trust her interest. That part of him did not believe that she wouldn't change her mind once he gave in to her.

So he avoided her—and with good reason.

The last time he had been at her side, even with the destruction all around them, he had wanted her desperately. When she had made the outrageous suggestion that he put his mouth and tongue on her, he had been filled with a raging desire. He had been unable to bear the idea of accepting her offer only to be laughed at or turned away. It was clear to him then that even being in her presence, he was too vulnerable to her. He could not laugh off her comments as he might have once before with a flirtatious female. Not with the way they made him yearn.

He cursed the contract that brought her there. The same contract that tied her to them for eight months so he was forced to skulk around his own domicile in order to avoid her. A deep growl rumbled out of him as he divested himself of his shirt and fell into bed. The viewing screen facing his bed, as programmed, immediately reacted to his presence and flickered on.

He expected to find his favorite vid stream waiting for him, the one thing he could use to escape his pressing desire for Crystal. Instead, he could lose himself in an impersonal stream of females beckoning an unknown lover to join them as they touched and teased themselves. There was no judgment, no interaction… just fantasy. Although more and more visions of Crystal interrupted the fantasy, drawing molten fire through his blood, he ignored them and pretended that it meant nothing.

Letting out a cleansing breath, he settled back comfortably on the bed, allowing his pants to fall open. He took himself into hand… and froze.

Pouty feminine faces filled the screen, but not those from a number of anonymous female pleasure actresses. It was all Crystal. Her hands slid down her clothed sides and along her thighs, hitching her shirt up. Not enough to bare skin, but to show the flared curves of her thighs and hips contained within her tight pants. His cock throbbed as his eyes fastened on the apex of her thighs encased in black fabric. She winked playfully, and a hand dipped under her shirt onto her belly…

He did not watch any more, but bolted up from the bed, closing his pants around his straining erection as he strode to the door. Anger fueled by hot, demanding arousal flooded through him as he stalked down the hall. He didn't know how she did it, but he knew without a doubt that she was responsible, just as she had been responsible for all her other pranks.

If this was a prank, then she had finally gone too far!

Exiting his room, he drew up short in surprise. Even from a distance, he could see that, at the other end of the corridor, her room stood open. As if he were expected.

He snarled silently. He probably was. Without hesitating further, he stormed toward her room, his pulse hammering beneath his skin.

The female knew exactly what she was doing even if she had no idea just what sort of male she was taunting and attempting to lure for some reason. The closer he got, the clearer he could see into her room. Her bed sat still along the same wall it always had, but what was different was the human female sprawled across it, a smile playing on her lips.

At that knowing look, he wanted to storm up to her side. He wanted to demand that she tell him her secrets, to pin her down until she yielded—to fuck her until neither of them could move and she was too exhausted to torment him any longer.

Crystal pushed herself up, her eyes meeting his.

"What an... unexpected surprise, Borth," she greeted him cheerfully.

He snorted in disbelief but did not stop coming at her until he had her backed up against the wall, his right knee on the soft bed as he pressed forward. He could smell the sweet, exotic perfume of her body as he dropped his head close, his breath fanning her skin.

"Do not play with me, female," he growled.

He watched as a shiver rolled over her, her breath hitching

slightly in response to the looming presence of his body and the caress of his words running over her. Even though it was a warning, she reacted to it with such pleasure that it gave him pause and spurred his own responses. His cock surged impatiently against his pants as he dropped his nose and nudged the exquisitely soft flesh there.

"You intruded into my privacy. Repeatedly."

Her head moved in a jerky nod, emphasizing the thrum of her excited pulse. Slowly, he extended his tongue and ran it along the fragile tempo, a thrill running through him as she squirmed, the heavy scent of arousal stirring around him.

"Yes," she gasped as he stroked his tongue along her throat again.

He leaned back just enough so that he could meet her eye. "I warned you away. I made every effort to spare you my attentions until you could be free of us. Why?"

An unreadable look flashed over her face before it disappeared, and she gave him a helpless look. "I don't know. I just want to be happy. I've been rejected several times… Did you know that? Maybe I couldn't bear the thought of being rejected again. And for some reason that even I can't quite understand, I want you. There's something here between us that I can feel."

He let his breath out in a painful hiss. There was something… He couldn't deny it. Even forcing distance could not mute it, not when it pulled him back and had him spying on her in secret. But neither did he want to consider that it might be more than lust. Lust he understood, and he could scent all over her skin. It was glorious, but it was impermanent, and it would not look beyond his imperfections. Lust would not hold her to him, and he was not sure he wanted it to.

"I am not like Grish. I cannot promise you a future."

Her small pink tongue swept over her lips, drawing all his attention.

"We have eight months to decide," she whispered. "Does there have to be a promise right away? Can't we just try and see if we can be a family?"

His eyes closed as he considered. Could he do that? Would he be strong enough to let her go once her fascination ended if he became attached?

A quiver shot through him as he opened his eyes and focused his gaze once more on her. "And if we do not mate... what will become of you then?"

He watched with interest as her throat worked and a weak smile pulled at her lips.

"I'll return to Earth."

He cocked his head, careful not to accidentally swipe her with his ganthli or its horns. "If you have been rejected so often, why did you not return home before now then?"

"There's not much of a home to return to," she replied quietly. "I didn't want to go back, but it seems this is my last chance. Apparently, the Mate Index Distribution Program is tired of losing money transporting me to grooms who decide not to keep me and demand refunds. If this is going to be it, Borth, then I want it to be something spectacular for as long as I have it. It'll have to last me a long time."

His lips turned up slightly, flattered despite himself that she put such weight on joining with them. "I am certain that it would not have to last you long before you found a human male. Someone more worthy of you."

Even as he said the words, he hated that they even fell from his tongue. Not only did they fill him with an inexplicable rage that she might give herself to another male after him, but her smile dropped away and her expression shuttered.

Running a hand through her hair, marveling at how large it appeared beside her head and how fine her hair was as the threads spilled between his fingers, he swept his hand down to cup her cheek and tilt her face to meet his eyes.

"I do not say these things to hurt you, but to reassure you. If you join with me now, it will not change anything. I will still not give any promises. I will not agree to mate and bind you to me."

A quiet sigh left her parted lips. "Borth, if this is about your leg…"

"Do not," he interrupted, his heart tightening in his chest. He did not want to hear false assurances about his disability. He did not want to hear her tell him that it is fine when it was not, when she hadn't seen him in the worst agony during the midwinter.

One soft hand ran along his jawline, playing among the small nubbed horns there before tracing up his cheek until he finally looked at her. She arched an eyebrow at him as her fingers continued to dance across his scales.

"Just this then… For now?"

"So long as you understand."

"I'll understand as long as you try. You don't have to make me any promises, nor will I try to force them from you… but don't ignore me any longer."

He narrowed his eyes on her. "Will you cease sabotaging our domicile?"

A charmingly crooked, cunning smile lit up her face.

"I promise nothing," she replied sweetly.

"Then I suppose my brother and I will have to keep you too tired to create mischief." He paused, a thought occurring to him. "You and Grish, have you…?"

She shook her head. "Not that I didn't want to. I'm pretty sure he wanted to as well, but he seemed determined to wait."

Borth grunted, feeling an overwhelming flood of emotion for his brother. Grish held back until he was certain that they would both be able to enjoy the pleasures of having Crystal there with them. Borth was still concerned that his brother would give his heart too quickly and too easily before Borth was ready—if he was ever ready. That his brother made that sacrifice gave him a certain peace about the arrangement that he hadn't felt until then.

Grish had not pushed and would not push him for more. He was letting Borth lead with as much as he was comfortable with. Only their crafty female demanded that he begin to move outside of what was comfortable and familiar since his retirement. She did it in such a way that, even if it drove him mad and infuriated him at times, he couldn't resent her.

Pushing more firmly up onto the bed, Borth hovered over Crystal, pausing long enough to give her one more chance to change her mind and back out. Although during the conversation, their arousal had ebbed, her arms opened to welcome him. One hand gripped a lower horn as she drew him, unresisting, to cover her. Dipping his head, he caught her lips with his, enjoying the taste of her on his tongue as he explored her.

The kiss went on, their tongues sliding together as they learned each other's flavors and pleasures as groans and pleased sighs broke the air. His body moved against her, his cock hard and aching without relief. He needed more.

Bending forward more, he sought to change his angle so to be able to part his pants when his knee spasmed. His body shuddering with pain, he reluctantly broke the kiss and pulled away. Turning his head, he glared down at his useless knee.

"I cannot…"

Her fingers pressed lightly to his lips, stemming his flow of self-castigating words. "Then don't. Tell me how you'd like me."

He looked up from his leg in surprise, meeting her earnest gaze, and was grateful that she saved his pride by not offering or demanding to take control. Instead, she surrendered it completely to him, waiting for his instruction as she stared up at him eagerly, her skin once more wearing the musky perfume of her desire.

Nodding, he stood, his fingers quickly separating the front seam of his pants.

"Lights off," he growled as he slipped the material off his hips.

The soft light of the moon filtered through the window as he settled on the bed. Just as he had once imagined, he covered his lower legs with the bedding. His cock was already swollen, stabbing proudly into the air. His balls tightened with a tingle of pleasure as he watched her disrobe until she stood naked beside the bed. Although he couldn't see the light sprinkle of freckles that a few days of sun had painted across her skin, he could make out the shadowed globes of her breasts and the lush curve of her thighs that hid her sex from sight.

"Come," he ordered.

It was only a whisper of movement, and then she was there, her body sliding over him. The slick heat of her sex settled against his abdomen, and she wiggled excitedly, her bottom brushing his cock. He let out a deep groan, fingers squeezing her thighs. Instead of pushing her back to cover his cock, he gave a short, demanding tug forward.

"First, I want to taste you. Come up here."

Crystal balked with uncertainty. "Umm, Borth, I'm kind of big for that."

He let out a bark of laughter. Odd that now of all times she would be uncertain. "You are tiny, female."

"You're not going to think that when I'm suffocating you."

He snorted at the idea.

"I do not worry about such things, nor should you. Now move."

She followed his demands until she settled her sex over his mouth. The scent of her soft, damp sex made his mouth water. Without hesitation, he gripped her legs to keep her in place as he ran his wide tongue from the base of her slit to the small pearl of flesh at its head. She jerked with a shallow gasp of surprise, but he did not let her up. Her flavor was unlike anything he had ever experienced. He immediately swiped his tongue again, harder this time, to draw up more of the intoxicating sweetness. A groan broke free from him, filled with urgency as she squirmed and bathed his tongue with her heat.

More!

CHAPTER 14

Crystal groaned and moved against Borth's mouth, her hips straining against the iron-hard grip of his hands locked upon them. His thick lips sucked on her sex and his long tongue stroked her as he worked her body. A soft whine trembled in her throat as she felt a quiver deep within her. She squirmed, attempting to chase the orgasm, but Borth kept her locked in place, leisurely, hungrily lapping at her until she wanted to scream in frustration. He was intentionally keeping her right on edge, playing with her, drawing out her arousal until her pussy was a slippery mess against his mouth as he eagerly licked and sucked it off.

"Borth, quit fucking with me and let me come," she panted with another twitch of her hips.

She felt his chuckle as much as heard it. He moved his mouth aggressively over her at her demand, a hungry growl vibrating against her sex as his tongue prodded her, swirling just inside of her channel in a loud slurping sound. Her hips arched against his hold, a cry tearing free from her as her muscles tightened. She ground against him, her sex clenching on air when suddenly his tongue disappeared and his mouth pulled hard on her clit. The sharp pleasure-pain shot through her, igniting her climax as her body trembled and bucked against him. He held tightly to her through it all, sucking on her clit alternating with long swipes of his tongue over her slit.

Crystal trembled against him, her clit overstimulated, sending sparks through her as his lips continued to toy with her. A sigh of relief escaped her when his mouth finally withdrew. She entertained the thought of collapsing on her side for only a moment before he lifted her easily into the air and moved her down his body until she felt the hot press of the head of his cock against her slick opening. He paused only for a moment, his fiery gaze meeting hers, before slowly lowering her, his sex pressing deep in a relentless drive.

His girth stretched her wide, and instinctively she bore against him, her pussy clenching as if attempting to fight out the large intrusion. Borth growled, his thumb pressing against her clit, and flicked it as he lifted his hips and shoved his way in. A fresh flow of arousal eased his way in by a couple of inches, but when it became apparent that he wasn't going to fit in any further, he drew back his hips and pumped into her repeatedly, each thrust taking him deeper within her as he continued to play with her clit.

Her breath burst out of her in pants as she moved against him, the penetration sending sparks of pleasure racing through her. She pushed down against his every thrust, determined to take more of him, demanding more pleasure. Her body quivered, a fine sheen of sweat on her skin when at last his cock nudged the mouth of her womb, and the scales of his belly pressed intimately against her.

She was fully seated on his massive cock. She instinctively clenched tightly around it, relishing in how full she felt, dragging a low, snarling groan from the male as his cock jerked within her.

His eyes blazed at her as he gave her a chastising look. "Keep that up and I will not restrain my rut," he bit out.

A spasm tightened her channel, making the head twitch hard within her. He hissed and pulled her down against him as he ground into her. She felt the first spurt of something warm that sent a tingly rush throughout her pussy like it was lit with electric pulses.

"What… what is that?" she whimpered as she felt desire claw through her.

She needed more of him. She didn't want to just be locked in place, no matter how good that felt. Her pussy creamed against him as she rocked back, enjoying the silky press of the fine scales covering his scrotum at the back of her sex. It was like a fire was set in her blood, demanding more. She needed to fuck, to be taken aggressively.

"Borth?"

His breath hissed out of him as he pulled back slightly and rammed back deep inside of her. The muscles of his forearm tightened. "You are fertile. It is my pre-breeding ejaculate to make you more needy and receptive to being bred," his deep voice rumbled. "It is a natural reaction to your pheromones. I am sorry," he grunted.

That sent up a mental red flag through her haze of need. "Sorry, for wha…?"

She felt something swell within her, pinching as it wedged tightly within her followed by more of the heat bathing her insides. She squirmed in shock and attempted to lift free, except the head of his cock wasn't sliding out of her. The peculiar-shaped head and the first inches following it were wedged tightly within her pussy. Pleasure tripped through her as the pulling sensation at the mouth of her channel.

She knew that if she tried hard, she could pull free. It might hurt, but she could do it—but the rush of pleasure overrode any concerns that she had at his words. Instead, she sank down on him while he snarled and yanked her back down, the hard stab of his cock making her cry out.

Fingers biting into her hips, Borth yanked her up and down against him, her clit bumping against his scales every time he bottomed out deep within her. She clung to his wrists, demanding more as she threw her head back and gasped between her moans and cries. His own deep grunts filled the air around them with nearly every thrust of his cock, his hips snapping eagerly, desperate, against her as that thick member shuttled back and forth. Every so often, she could feel more hot sprays within her, amping up her pleasure, making her more receptive, until he broke into a hard, ceaseless rut.

He snarled as he shifted, seemingly no longer cognizant of his knee as he pushed up onto them, her body falling back to hang even as her thighs clamped around him.

"More…" she snarled. She hardly recognized her voice, but the need was making her wild. She growled and clawed at him, demanding his full rut. She didn't want him to temper it. "Give me more, Borth. Rut me. Fuck me now. Gods, why can't I feel you like I did? Please," she whimpered with a desperate squirm against him.

She needed the fire within her assuaged.

A low, bassy sound erupted from the bony crest on his head in response, and he pressed forward. His hips drove against her in desperation, his scrotum slapping hard against her bottom. The bed rattled beneath them, but it still wasn't enough. She clawed against his forearms and arched her body.

"*Katna*, is everything okay…?" Grish's voice trailed off at the doorway to end on a husky groan.

She turned her head toward him and blinked against the fog of lust. Grish was stripping off his clothes and striding toward her. Her eyes fixed on his swelling cock, the wedged head seeming to inflate slightly as she watched. He wanted her too, and gods, did she need him. She needed both of them!

"Borth, is she ready?" he rasped.

The growl that came from Borth was unintelligible, his cock spewing inside of her with every thrust now.

"Locked in," Borth panted, his entire body trembling.

Grish nodded. "You should have told me that you were going to do this, and I would have been here. Lay back, brother, I will help her and you. We will break the heat."

Borth turned his head and snarled aggressively at his brother's touch but relented with a nod. Crystal cried out as the angle shifted, and she was draped over him, the ease of his thrusting making her scramble against him. His tail came up and laid against her back, capturing her against him despite her efforts. She was only vaguely aware of Grish settling behind her, but when the head of his cock pressed against her opening, nudging alongside Borth's dick already filling her, she paused.

He wouldn't…

Grish pressed forward, his cock sliding against Borth's as he pressed deep within her pussy. His hand stroked against her rump as he thrust deep until both males were wedged within her. Crystal felt an upwelling of panic.

There was no way her body was meant to do these things!

"Relax, *katna*," he growled. "There is a reason Terils mate with paired males. The females need both of us as much as we need it. This will not harm you. As our mate, you need it. So does he."

Crystal felt Borth's cock leap within her as Grish pulled back and drove into her again, breath fanning her neck as she was pressed between them. Her clit rubbed against Borth's scales as the male beneath her strained to keep himself planted deep within her as Grish began to work her pussy from behind.

A shudder rippled through her as the males began to move in tandem, their heads pressing together, slipping against each other inside her. Borth's arms came up behind her shoulders, keeping her pressed flat to him as he jerked her down with every press of his hips, forcing Grish to pick up his pace.

A low, growling moan sounded behind her as Grish's gentle rhythm fell apart, his strokes turning desperate, his cock now also jerking inside of her. She felt the press of his lips against the nape of her neck, a show of affection in the rising waves of heat and need. He thrust again and again until a bellow escaped him. One hand reached past her to grab onto one of Borth's horns, yanking the male roughly so that his cock twitched within her.

All three of them groaned. One of Borth's hands came to grip Grish's horn as well, and Crystal barely had time to draw in a breath before they were riding her, their bodies moving against hers in a tempo that made color explode before her eyes. A tightness that had built through Borth's rutting swelled inside her as Grish also became locked, their cocks butting into her, pushing her higher, closer to the relief she needed.

When at last her climax hit, she screamed, her pussy spasming hard. Her males trumpeted their pleasure as their seed spurted into her. They strained and grunted as they gave it up, cocks pressing deep. They were still jerking as she came down from her orgasm, their cocks still inside. Crystal blinked and swallowed reflexively. Her throat felt raw.

"Wow…" she rasped

Grish pressed a kiss to the back of her shoulder. "I apologize, *katna*. Normally it's not so hard on a female. Borth shouldn't have joined with you without me, or at least with me nearby. Terils are not designed to mate in pair bonds. It is not healthy for us, as you can see. Both of you could have been injured if I had not heard you."

The male in question turned his head, his breath coming out in a weak chuckle. "Perhaps so, brother, but it would have been a fine way to go."

She couldn't argue with that.

CHAPTER 15

Grish scowled at the crowds as they pressed in close. Although Yaturnak wasn't as large as Intakfell, he was disturbed and all too aware of just how many males were too close to his female. It was a strange sensation, since he had never considered himself possessive before. In all his past dealings with females, he had been prone to being easygoing and so lacking in any jealous traits that it had frustrated some females who expected more reaction from him.

But this was different.

Even though they had yet to mate her, as far as Grish was concerned, Crystal was *theirs*. He could now appreciate the way other males he had known had reacted around their mates. Territorial, protective. Even though he knew from the scent of their female's unchanged pheromones that they hadn't bred her, he paced behind her as menacingly as if she were carrying his young. Of the two of them, Borth was more relaxed, but he was on alert as well, even if he wasn't snarling at any male who breached their personal space like Grish was.

Who would have believed that Borth would be the mellower of them when it came to their female?

And there was no question, despite his brother's resistance to establishing a mating claim until he was certain that she would remain with them, that Borth was just as attached as he was.

Grish's expression softened as he glanced down at their female. Crystal did not appear to even notice the other males. She was chewing her bottom lip as she looked over the list that Talimia had sent to her datapad.

He had been surprised to learn that the Wanit female offered to teach her how to cook. Although Nargis was friendly with them, Wanit females were known to prefer the company of their own kind. They would socialize to a certain extent, but not to the point where they would want to be around them regularly. Certainly not as often as a daily cooking lesson. Nargis had been equally surprised, but quite pleased when they had left. It still had been difficult to believe, and for days, Grish waited for the female to comm to make her excuses.

That had not happened. Instead, Crystal had received a list early in the morning. She didn't greet it with excitement, but rather with determination, like she was setting out to conquer something. She still had that look to her as she read the list with only the occasional thoughtful wrinkle marring her brow.

"I hope you guys know what some of this stuff is," she said as she dodged oncoming foot traffic, "because looking at this is like trying to decipher a bizarre encryption code."

Grish leaned forward, eyes scanning the list, and he nodded. "Yes, that will all be easy enough to find. A few of those things we grow and can put into storage for your use."

"Really? We do?" She gave the list a curious look. "Which ones?"

He chuckled as he pointed them out on the list. "Mandars, gurek, effontal, saprili, and vintir." He rubbed his chin. "I see you have yamril milk on your list. Perhaps we will see about getting a milking animal to keep at the farm. We intended to procure live-stock but never came to do it."

"Oh, like what?" she asked, glancing up from her datapad.

"Gorthals," Borth said with a grin that had been absent from his face since his pains had returned to him.

"What's a gorthal?"

"Fine mounts. Strong, fast animals suitable for carrying a large male such as us. And they are very smart," Grish explained. "The Mintigi breed and raise them as work and transport animals. Borth and I have often spoke of looking at some local stock."

"Then why haven't you? Are they really expensive?" she asked, her list forgotten with her curiosity piqued.

He loved that about their female. She had an insatiable mind.

He shook his head. "No, nothing like that. We do very well and have plenty of money and could buy several if we were so inclined. The reason we haven't is more because we rarely bother to come into town. We order what few supplies we need to be delivered. However, now that you are with us, it seems a better idea to allow you to pick for yourself what you would like."

"You're going to set me loose in your house and let me do as I like?" she asked, smiling.

"Why not? It could not be any worse than the lack of effort that we have put toward it."

"It is a bit bare," she agreed. "Well, then, that settles it. We'll give the house a new look, and this would be a good opportunity to look at some gorthals." She glanced down at her body. "And maybe some new clothes, so I'm not cycling through the same three outfits."

"You did arrive with surprisingly little. I have never seen a female with so few clothes," Grish admitted. "I thought perhaps it was a personal preference of yours, so refrained from commenting on it."

"No, it was more out of necessity," she sighed. "It's a long story, and I—"

"Ugaar... Grish and Borth Ugaar," a voice interrupted.

Grish suppressed a groan. This was why they seldom went into town. Terils stood out among other species, and he hated fending off the representatives of the Megaraisi Corporation who held offices in town. After many communities had ousted them for the disastrous effects of their heavy equipment use, they had turned with a greedy eye toward the small independent farms. Turning, he leveled an irritated look at the Calystii standing behind him. His irritation heightened when he scented his mate's fear and heard her startled gasp.

"What do you want?"

The male's glance lingered on Crystal thoughtfully but returned to him with an ingratiating smile. "Allow me to introduce myself. I am Danya, a representative for the Megaraisi Corporation..."

"Not interested," he interrupted as they pushed by the smaller male, their female sheltered between them. "Now, if that is all, we have other things that requires our attention."

"Perhaps your female would be of another opinion," the male said. His hard gaze landed on Crystal, rousing Grish's anger. "After all, females are far more reasonable about things that are in their best interest. It can be a bastion of safety... Is that not correct?"

Their mate shrank back from the male, her eyes darting around nervously. Grish growled and stepped between the Calystii and his female.

"Is that a threat?" Borth snarled from the other side, his tail slapping the ground with a thud.

The male sniffed and glared at them. "I cannot believe I have been reduced to this... dealing with males such as yourselves. Brutish, undisciplined primitives."

Grish sneered. "You Calystii like to forget that Telif Prime was one of the founding members of the Intergalactic Union, while your species was still fumbling around your own solar system and applauding yourselves for conquering the Lorgors."

"I see there's no reasoning with you, as usual. Very well. I shall report to command. There is an Imperial ship that will be happy to receive my report, I think."

"Grish…" Crystal whispered.

He set a calming hand on her shoulder and steered her away from the male. It disturbed him to see their fierce female frightened, but clearly there was some reason behind it. Although the Calystii Imperial Family had considerable might behind them, most Calystii were harmless.

"Do not worry, *katna*. He is, as you humans say, all bark and no bite. He cannot hurt you, especially not with two Teril males protecting you. He is nothing."

"But he's going to tell the ship…"

"And what would they care? The Imperial Family is invested in the Megaraisi Corporation but not so deeply that they care about every little insult directed toward the corporation."

"It is not that simple," she groaned. "Look, there's something I have to tell you…"

"When we return to our domicile, you can tell us everything you need. Until then, let us focus on our purpose for being here and not let one lone male ruin our day," Borth suggested as he took up position at her other side, his hand sweeping down her arm in a comforting gesture.

She took a deep breath and nodded, though reluctantly. "Yeah, you're right. I'm sure there's nothing that can be done about it at this very minute anyway."

"And it would take time for even an Imperial ship to arrive on the far outskirts of Antari Minor. We will deal with any problem, if it comes at all," he reassured her softly.

Crystal, even standing protected between them, appeared so vulnerable that it made his heart ache. Despite her fear, she made an obvious effort to marshal her strength and gave him a weak smile. She blew out a breath and lifted her datapad once more.

"First thing on the list is a fatty borhawl flank."

As they wove through the crowds, Crystal seemed to relax again as she focused on her task. They filled baskets with cuts of meat, fruits, vegetables, and spices that Grish had never seen before. A few weren't even on the list but were added to their pile because of their female's joy over discovering them.

At first, the Mintigi who ran the largest number of stalls in the market were cautious toward their female, treating her warily, though respectfully, while pitching their sales to either Grish or Borth. He knew that it was likely due to the imposing presence of two large Teril males flanking her, but once it became obvious who had the most influence over their purchases, the Mintigi changed tactics.

They soon began to eagerly present their wares to her, showing her their finest pottery made of the rare clay found only in hidden reservoirs. Others offered cooked samples of meat, pointing out what spices seasoned the meat best and the choice parts of different animals that they had butchered.

Although the Mintigi didn't run farms, they were expert hunters, and their nomadic lifestyle was suited to their herds. With the high-tech cooling units they acquired, they made their clans profitable by largely doing as they had done for generations. Every week, they came to the market with the choicest fresh meats, select beasts, and beautifully made items.

From the Mintigi, Grish was able to arrange transportation of a milking yamril to be delivered to their property the next day. The female tossed her white head, sporting a webbed crest and horns, as she made a harsh trilling sound. Crystal had watched in fascination and laughed when the animal attempted to take a bite out of her clothing.

And then there were the gorthals. They had finished their shopping, paying for their items and arranging transportation for items that were too large or too delicate to take home with them, such as the large collection of dishware that Crystal selected. The gorthal breeders were their last stop among the stalls. The large animals immediately craned their heads to calmly watch their approach.

"They're *huge*," Crystal observed in awe. "Like a Clydesdale on steroids."

Grish raised an eyebrow at the odd descriptor but gestured to the animals with a sound of pleasure. "You see why we wanted to acquire mounts such as these."

"Yeah, one could probably carry both of you," she laughed. "What are you going to do by yourself on one? They're enormous! I know Terils are big, but that one over there could hold all three of us and still have room if we squeezed together."

A sound rumbled from his chest as he contemplated the idea. "That has some very distinct possibilities for pleasure," he said in a low voice as he nuzzled the sensitive skin at her neck.

"Ah, you have picked the finest male of my herd," a Mintigi male said happily as he came over to their side. His short frame was wider than most of his species, but his eyes gleamed appreciatively as if accessing just how much he might be able to get from them. "He has sired a number of quality gorthals. If you are looking for a breeding male, there is none better."

Grish hummed to himself as he inspected the animal. "Aggression? I would need three mounts and do not wish to lose animals due to the bad temperament of one."

The animal lowered a large, wooly head, his thick, tapered muzzle brushing across Grish's chest as the gorthal scented him before lowering its head further to inspect Crystal. His female snorted out a happy laugh as the gorthal repeated the same action, curiously mouthing at her hair and loose clothing as he inspected her.

"He is a good, stable animal," the breeder assured, smiling at the enthusiastic way Crystal patted the animal. "I would not recommend penning him with other males if you wish to breed him. He prefers to have his females to himself. But if you are just planning to keep him as a mount, he isn't aggressive with other members of his herd."

"Why do they have large horns growing out of their heads? They'd look like giant wooly unicorns if it didn't sweep back like that over the top of their heads."

The Mintigi made a sound of pleasure at the question, pride puffing out his chest. "The horns are not normally that long. That's an example of very fine breeding. Both males and females have them. It makes them sensitive to changes in the energy of their environment. They have been able to detect and move their herds, and subsequently our people, away from appearances of awepi before they emerge from the mountains, as well as warning us of approaching storms. It's also an important part of their ability to move around obstacles. Their eyesight is poor, so they rely on echolocation. The males, who develop larger horns, also use them in dominance displays and to fend off predators from the herds. As do the hard spurs jutting out from their jaws and the corners of their mouths."

"Amazing," she whispered, her eyes wide as they skimmed over the animals. They landed on the male once more in apprecia-tion. "I'll be sure to remember that. Oh, one more question."

"Yes?"

"If I sent out a signal in electric pulses, coded to a specific pattern and rhythm, can they be trained to respond to them?"

"How clever! Yes, I imagine they would. My people sometimes use vibrational mechanisms to bring in our herds, so I imagine it would work the same way."

The male smiled as she input the information on her datapad.

"We will take him, and two others of our choice. Will you be able to arrange delivery?" Grish asked.

"Absolutely! You have picked a magnificent male. Please take your time picking out two others. I will give you a very good price for the three of them. Might I make a suggestion, however, for your little female?"

Grish and Borth exchanged a look. To that extent, normally exchanges with Mintigi were made with a mind on credits. Borth nodded, and Grish gestured for the male to continue. The Mintigi disappeared into a cluster of animals, bringing out a smaller golden animal with a large horn.

"This is an umprenal gorthal. Smaller than the standard breed, as you can see, and also of milder temperament. These are the animals that our clans use as mounts. We rarely sell them to offworlders… but I like your female's curiosity and her appreciation of my animals, so I'm willing to offer him. Your human is small, and I would be saddened to learn that she became injured falling from a larger animal. I also have a feeling that she will need further protection. The umprenal gorthal can be a fierce protector of their riders. I do not like the way that Calystii is looking at her."

Alarm shot through Grish as he turned in the direction that the Mintigi indicated. He was certain he saw the sleek shining scales of a Calystii male slipping back into the crowd, but he couldn't be certain.

Grunting, Grish waited on edge as Borth made his selection. Once the credits were exchanged, he did not hesitate to rush his family away from the market. The situation with the Calystii appeared to be more serious than he thought.

Just what had their female stumbled into?

CHAPTER 16

"And then Robby disappeared, leaving a clear trail to my home and every Calystii on the Imperial ship apparently certain that I had done it," Crystal said with a long, weary sigh. After so many years of running, it felt good to speak of it, to share her burden with someone else.

Not just someone else, but the Teril males protecting her.

"Why did you not report it?" Borth asked, his brow drawn down with concern.

Crystal sighed and rubbed her face with her hands, only moderately comforted by Matida's head pressing into her lap. There were times when she asked herself the same question, and it always came down the same problem: she had nothing that would encourage the government to support her against a Calystii Imperial Army. In the larger scheme of things, she was a very tiny fish in a huge intergalactic ocean.

"And tell them what? That I sometimes walk on the wrong side of the law and my boyfriend decided to be incredibly stupid against my advice? Would I beg my government to hide me and protect me when the Calystii are determined to get what they want and believe that I have it? They probably would have tossed me right to them, begging forgiveness because some idiot on Earth stole from an Imperial ship."

Grish grimaced but nodded in agreement. "She is right," he grumbled to his brother. "The Calystii make a game of threatening newer planets in the Union if they cross them to establish their dominance. Theft would give them the perfect reason to retaliate if the government chose to protect her. They obviously want whatever this male—Robby—has very much to pursue her this long. No doubt they have her likeness spread among them, waiting for the alert."

"One they now have because of that male, Dayna," Borth said bitterly. "The entire Calystii Imperial Army is likely on their way, heading for our door. They could demolish our entire farm with almost no effort."

Crystal winced. Why hadn't she considered that?

"That is why you signed up for the Mate Index, is it not?" Borth challenged, his eyes hot with anger.

"Well," she hedged, "I didn't so much as sign up as hack my way in and process my paperwork myself for an immediate departure from Earth."

"So it was all a scam. You are not looking for a mate, but for someone to protect you," he shot back.

She gaped at him. *That's completely unfair!*

"No! I mean, yeah, I wanted to hide, but I wasn't trying to trick anyone. I wanted somewhere I could settle and live peacefully with a mate."

"It was selfish! And unfortunately, we were the only ones who have yet to be able to get rid of you fast enough to avoid being targeted by the Calystii Imperial Family!" Borth shouted. "Do you realize you could ruin everything we have here? Eight cycles to destroy revolutions of work."

Grish sighed and shook his head. "There were no required eight cycles. It was never in the contract, brother. She spoke a falsehood that day, and I went along with it because I was desperate to find happiness for us. I never imagined it would come to this."

"I will not tolerate a deceptive mate. There is no knowing what all she lied about. She could even be lying about the Calystii. She admits to doing illegal work, so it's possible. Regardless, we cannot trust her. She leaves first thing in the morning!" Borth growled as he spun away, limping heavily on his bad leg.

Crystal's mouth dropped open, the dig quite obvious. She snapped it closed again, eyes narrowing angrily on him as he left the room. She swallowed back angry tears and dropped her head.

What use was there to cry about it? She was getting rejected again—only this time she actually cared enough for it to truly hurt. She felt Grish's hand come down on her arm comfortingly, and she jerked away from it.

He was going to throw her out. She didn't want comfort from either of the Ugaar brothers.

He froze, and his hand dropped away. His voice was heavy with sorrow as he spoke, but she ignored it.

"I am sorry, *katna*. I could not continue the lie with all this coming to light. Perhaps Borth will change his mind after he has had a chance to think it over. If not, at least you can go home and make a new life until I can talk him around to putting aside his anger. No one will know where you have gone. We will just say that you left for a vacation offworld, if anyone asks."

"Sure," she muttered, pulling away from him. "I think I'll go get some sleep. I imagine we'll be leaving early in the morning."

"Yes, probably," he agreed sadly.

Her arms wrapped around her chest, she lifted her head and glared. "I hate you for this." She felt a stirring of guilt at the way he winced in pain but pushed on. "You made me care and want to be here and have a life with you, and now you're ripping it all away. You could have left well enough alone. I could have enjoyed peace for eight months while I got my shit in order and then I would have been out of here. You made me want and imagine more than that."

"*Katna…*" He stepped forward, his hand reaching out for her, but she neatly evaded his touch.

"No, you don't get to call me that. I'm not your dearest, or your anything. Not anymore. You don't get to call me that before you throw me away."

"I am not throwing you away," he growled in frustration. "I just need time to get this figured out. I still want you. *We* still want you. Borth is angry. We will figure it out, I promise."

She nodded once, refusing to meet his gaze.

It didn't matter anyway. If she returned to Earth, she would be in jail. Once that happened, it wouldn't be like they could just stroll to the jail and be all, *"Oopsie, we changed our mind. Our bad."* She couldn't depend on Borth to be able to figure out what he wanted and needed, not when he still held deep doubts about them.

It was time to face facts. Her time was running out. She needed to get out of there and lie low somewhere until she figured out her next steps.

Crystal stalked to her room. She went immediately to the storage panel on the wall and fetched her backpack. It had served her well over the years. No reason to break with tradition now. Carrying it over to the bed, she began to pack her things.

She glanced casually at the bags still sitting on her bed from where she had set them after returning from the market. Her stomach soured at the sight. Several loose tunics and pants were stretched out besides the bags, but she didn't reach for them. Instead, she dug into the bags for the snacks she had picked out.

She didn't want to take anything from the house with her, but she wasn't so foolish as to leave food behind, not when they would put something in her belly while she was traveling. Hopefully the guys would be able to get their money back for everything else. Or maybe give her new things to Talimia.

The datapad sitting on the bedside table tempted her, but she paused only long enough to fish out the ear transponders and set them beside it. It pained her to leave the gifts, the things that Grish provided for her to be able to maintain contact with the rest of the world. Still… it could serve one last purpose to suit her needs.

Picking it up, she transferred schematics of the surrounding land and property lines to her comm and overrode the security systems, providing herself with a forty-five-minute window to get off the property. They would never know that she left until she was long gone. They would have no information to give to the Calystii if they came looking, whether it was days or months down the road.

It could only buy her more time.

Initializing the override, Crystal crept from the room into the darkened house. As part of the override, the lights did not activate as she made her way to the front door. Everything was quiet, as it should be. Keying the manual override, she shrugged her pack more comfortably in place and waited as the door slid open.

She was tempted to take one last look, but shook off the impulse as she stepped out the door into the night.

Although she had no real plan, she had an idea of at least where she might seek some help for a day. Talimia also had an intergalactic comm system. If she could talk her friend into letting her use it, just maybe she could arrange passage off the planet. She didn't really have much of value, and her credits were dangerously low, but she could probably make a series of illegal transfers to give her enough credits to get off the planet. Perhaps she could see about enlisting her services to a patron somewhere. Someone had to have some use for her skills.

Once she was far enough from the house that she was certain that the light from her comm wouldn't be seen, she pulled up Talimia's contact information and opened the comm line between them on a secure frequency. It didn't take long for the Wanit to answer. Her friend's confused expression cleared immediately when she saw her.

"Crystal, where are you? Is everything all right?"

"Well enough. I'll explain later. I am coming through the southeastern edge of your property line. Would it be okay if I stopped there and used your comm system?"

"Of course, but I thought we were meeting later for your cooking lesson."

Crystal closed her eyes, unhappy to disappoint or hurt her new friend. Dredging up a smile, she shrugged.

"We will have to reschedule, if that's okay? There are a few things I need to take care of, and I'm not entirely sure when I'll be able to do it."

"I understand. We will arrange to do it later when you are settled again. In the meantime, of course you are welcome to come by and use my comm system. It was one of the few luxuries I insisted on when we left Wanmira, so it is decent."

"Thank you. I really appreciate it," she said quietly.

"Have you eaten?"

Crystal shook her head. "Not since this afternoon."

"Okay, I will warm the evening meal and have it ready when you arrive."

"Thank you, Talimia. You're such a good friend."

"You will tell me what is happening when you arrive—right?"

"Yeah, I'll tell you," Crystal said wearily.

The Wanit nodded and signed off, leaving Crystal to her thoughts as she made her way through the shadows of the orchard. It was eerie, especially with the flickering lights of the butterfly-like entigs fluttering around the trees.

Since arriving, she had never walked more than a few yards away from the house, other than her trip to town with Borth and Grish. Being out so far from the house on an alien world was new and frightening. Thankfully, it wasn't a long walk, and within the hour, she was being pulled into Talimia's warm house with Nargis watching groggily.

"Now remember, not a word that she's here," the female hissed to her mate. "You know the rules. Besides, if she wanted them to know where she was, she would have told them."

Nargis agreed reluctantly before shuffling off to bed, leaving them alone in the kitchen with only one last unhappy look in their direction before he disappeared down the hall.

"I'm sorry. I didn't mean to interrupt your routine. I know it's late," Crystal said quietly as she sat at the table.

Talimia waved her apology off. "It is not that. Do not worry. Nargis hates to keep secrets from his friends, but if you are here without them that means that they have done something stupid. The hunt has very specific rules in our culture. If they have offended and wish to make amends, then they must endure the trials of the hunt as well to prove themselves worthy once again." Talimia leaned forward soberly, placing a bowl in front of her. "Did they offend you?"

"They're assholes. I'm better off without them," Crystal said around a bite of the hot, filling food.

Talimia grinned. "Yes, of course they are."

Crystal returned her smile and settled more comfortably at the table. "I appreciate you doing this for me—and this food. It's very good."

"We are friends. Of course I would help you. More than one Wanit of my line has helped another bury a body a time or two."

Choking back a laugh, Crystal looked fondly upon the female. "You're a good friend, but I hope it won't come to that."

"Of course not. Burying bodies is a messy, foul-smelling, and overall, quite unpleasant task." Talimia laughed. "I do admit that I hope your males are successful in their hunt. I do not wish to lose another friend."

"You will never lose me. I'll comm as often as possible regardless of where I am."

"You will?" Talimia asked softly, a vulnerable expression descending over her features. There was a shade of doubt there that pained Crystal. The female had been hurt a lot by friends and family. She would not add to that.

"Yes, I will," she whispered.

The Wanit smiled shakily, blinking back her tears. "I am glad. Now hurry and eat so I can show you to the comm system. It is quite splendid," she said as she dashed a hand over her eyes. "I also have a little gift for you that should help you during the hunt."

"Thank you," Crystal said softly.

In less than an hour, she was linked, her mind cast about virtual space, sinking once more in the familiarity. She should have been elated to be back. It shouldn't have felt lonely drifting through cyberspace. There were countless people out there, moving in and out of the intergalactic system, who she could easily reach and touch at the drop of a hat.

Yet for once that thought didn't comfort her.

No one else was *them*.

She shook away the morose feeling. They had pushed her away. She had to be fine with that. She had no one but herself once she left Talimia's house. She knew that her friend would ask her to stay, but she wouldn't. Lingering only increased the risk that someone would find out that she had been there and alert the Calystii Imperial Fleet to that fact.

She needed to get to work.

Drifting deeper into the system, she wasn't sure how long she was there but felt a surge of elation when she found exactly what she was looking for. A buried, encrypted ad looking for an experienced technician with coding and encryption skills, among other specifics. Although she wasn't as on top of things as perhaps some of the more elite coders among the alien races, she pinged the ad and was gratified when she received an immediate response. They would meet her at Intakfell and arrange immediate transport from there to their homeworld of Lorgoon, courtesy of the Lorgor uprising.

A whispered breath of surprise left her as she left the systems and dropped the virtual visor away from her eyes before returning it to the small protective case in her pack. The Lorgor uprising. The irony of the situation wasn't lost on her.

"Well," Talimia said. "Did you find something?"

"Oh yes, I definitely did," Crystal chuckled.

Her friend's relived grin spread over her face. "Wonderful. What can I do?"

"Well," Crystal said slowly, "do you have a way to help me get to Intakfell?"

"Of course! I will transport you personally."

"Talimia!" Nargis shouted from the door of the comm room. Crystal wasn't sure when exactly he arrived at that spot, since last she had seen he had been intent on returning to their room. The outrage on his face meant that he at least arrived just in time to hear his mate's offer.

The female directed a steely look at her mate. "The law of the hunt, Nargis," she reminded him once more in a hard voice as she led Crystal away into another room.

Sleep was elusive, despite the comfort of a plush bed and knowing that her friend wouldn't let anyone disturb her. Still, Crystal's mind was restless as it continued to circle. The offered position within the heart of a resistance movement where her skills would be valued and depended on warred with images of Grish and Borth and their regular routines and the upgrades that they had discussed as they cuddled together in bed. She felt the strain in her mind and heart, and it followed her into her restless slumber and into the waking hours the next morning as she prepared to leave on the flyer with Talimia.

CHAPTER 17

*B*orth was exhausted. Sleep had eluded him late into the night despite his attempts to distract himself. Nothing had worked, and when it finally came, he had slept fitfully. His heart felt heavy, and there was no wondering as to the cause.

He rubbed one hand down his face.

He needed to apologize to Crystal and pray she would forgive him. He had been caught by surprise, but he never should have said what he had.

Discovering that the threat from the Calystii was not just a couple of males that had to be dealt with but an Imperial Army of Caysa had alarmed him. That her presence with them was all a part of an elaborate ruse to escape had cut deep. Made him question everything. Even more so when it became apparent that the lies had not stopped there.

The only thing he could think was that they weren't equipped to fight an army, and if she had lied and kept secrets, how could he know that anything between them had been true?

It hurt, and he had reacted quickly in order to protect himself.

Now that all that anger and confusion had ebbed out of him, he was left with regret and worry. Regardless of what brought her to their door, there had been no lie in her touch or in any part of her life with them. Outside of tricking him into giving her a chance to fit into their lives, she had been blunt and straightforward about what she wanted from the first and pursued it relentlessly and unapologetically.

His lips quirked in a ghost of a smile.

It drove him mad, but he admired that persistence and forthrightness that had colored their relationship. She hadn't slipped away to find a more convenient target when she had the perfect opening to do just that. No, she had stubbornly stuck to him, asserting her place with them, and had enthusiastically shared his passion.

He could not even fault her for falsifying her documents. Despite his paranoia, he knew that it was a smart decision on her part. It was just odd that they were still pursuing her. He had never heard of the Calystii chasing this long. Not even pirates who plundered Calystii ships were hounded for more than a few cycles. That the Imperial family was still hunting Crystal after revolutions weighed on his mind, disturbing him throughout the night.

What could the male possibly have stolen that would have triggered such a massive hunt for it? That was the one thing he could not work through.

Borth frowned and pushed up from the bed to pace over to his bedroom window. His brow drew low as his eyes scanned the rear fields. For once, looking upon them did not bring him peace. Nor did it offer any answers.

Whatever it was, it was unlikely that the human stole a treasure or credits from the Imperial ship. The Calystii royals had plenty of those to spare. So this human, Robby, had to have stolen something detrimental, something that they wanted back very much.

That left them with only one option. They would have to hunt down the male and arrange a trade. The thief for Crystal's freedom.

It would not be easy, but it was not impossible.

Borth cracked his knuckles, allowing himself a moment to enjoy the fantasy of snapping Robby in half for all the misery he had inflicted on their female. Borth would not kill the male—after all, he did them a favor by leaving Crystal. Sparing him would repay that debt.

But that did not mean he couldn't take pleasure in slapping the human around a little to teach him the error of his ways. No permanent damage done, as a special thank you.

But first, Borth needed to apologize to Crystal. Once that was accomplished—and she hopefully forgave him—he would see if she had any ideas of where Robby might hide and any useful information on the male that might give them a clue where to locate him. One thing Borth was certain of: the male would not be on Earth. With Earth's infantile tech, the Calystii would have located him and terminated their search for Crystal.

Unfortunately, there were a number of dark pits into which the scum of the universe could escape to avoid being found. Which brought him right back around to how difficult their task was going to be.

A low, frustrated growl vibrated in Borth's throat. He needed to focus on one task at a time. Although the Calystii were concerning, Crystal was more important right now. His tail thumped the floor as he strode toward the door.

No sense in putting it off. The hour was still early, but it could not wait.

Leaving his room, he headed for hers at the end of the corridor and placed his hand on the comm panel. A soft beep let him know that the comm was open, and he took a breath to steady to himself. He could repair the damage he had done.

"Crystal, open the door... please," he tacked on quickly.

Silence met his request. It was not just quiet, but unnaturally so.

He frowned and leaned toward the door, straining to listen for rustling bedding or the creak of movement from within. There was nothing, not even a sigh of breath from someone disturbed in their sleep.

"Borth, what are you doing?" Grish's voice came from behind him.

Glancing back, he saw his brother standing midway in the corridor as if he had been merely passing through when he halted in place. Grish was fully dressed, wearing a perplexed look on his face as he raised one heavy brow ridge. Borth was well aware that he likely looked awful. The lack of sleep was, no doubt, a bad look paired with his rumpled clothes from yesterday. He scowled back, his arms crossing over his chest.

"You are up early."

Grish inclined his head in the affirmative and stepped toward him. "The gorthal breeder arrived early so I went out to meet him and get the animals settled. I decided to let Crystal sleep while I saw to the matter, and a few other personal ones, before I woke her. There is no reason to disturb her, I will take her to Intakfell shortly."

The latter was said without emotion, his brother's expression so blank and subdued that Borth felt the uncomfortable bite of guilt.

"The animals traveled well?" he asked evasively.

Grish nodded again. "Of course. The Mintigi is an excellent breeder. All three arrived in perfect condition." He hesitated and shrugged. "We will have to think of what to do with the umprenal. It is too small for either of us to have use for, but I did not have the heart to return him to the breeder. There is a chance we may need him if you ever wish to try again with acquiring a mate."

A flash of annoyance rose in Borth, and he leveled a glare on his brother. Crystal had not yet left their home and the male was already thinking ahead of replacing her.

As if Borth would agree to any such thing!

"You will do no such thing," he snarled, his chest puffing up with anger. "You will not be taking our female to Intakfell. You will not be turning her over to other males to claim. And you most certainly will not be speaking of giving her umprenal to another female or replacing her."

Grish suddenly smiled, his body relaxing. "Glad you've come to your senses. I have been spending much of my time while settling the animals trying to figure out how to make you see sense without doing any further physical damage to you. Your head is thick, brother."

"Perhaps so," Borth muttered. "But not so thick that I would be foolish enough to let our mate leave."

Grish let out a long, low whistle.

"Our mate now, is she?" he asked cheerfully. "This is better than I expected. Were you not the one who was insisting on taking things slowly just days ago?"

Borth glared at the other male. "You are enjoying this."

"Immensely," Grish agreed with a deep chuckle. "But not nearly as much as I will enjoy watching you beg her for her forgiveness for being—what was it?—a complete and utter shit?"

"I will do whatever is necessary," Borth grumbled, his attention once more returning to their female's door. "You may laugh if you like, but alone in my room, imagining our domicile without her in it... It is easy to play with rules and dance around each other until you realize it is going to be gone and you will never get it back."

Grish sobered and shook his head. "I thought for sure that you would hold onto your anger. Last night you were so sure she had deceived you into caring for her. I am relieved I did not have to beat the revelation into you for you to see beyond your pain."

A snort left Borth in answer to Grish's observation. "She was far too persistent to be anything but earnest. Besides, all she had to do was go to Yaturnak or return to Intakfell to find an easier arrangement with a lone male who would be grateful to have her. She did not want two mates when she arrived, and certainly not an uncooperative male. She did not treat me like I was undesirable," he admitted.

"At last, you see," Grish announced, his arms outstretched dramatically in an eye-roll worthy performance. The male dropped his arms and grinned cheerfully. "So, what is your plan now to gain our female's forgiveness?"

"I plan to apologize—and to explain. If she would respond to her comm and let me in," he muttered, glaring at the closed door. A thought occurred to him then, and he glanced over at Grish and raised a brow ridge. "Did you see any trace of her anywhere when you returned to the house?"

Grish shook his head. "The domicile has been silent all morning. As I said, I assumed that she was asleep still. She was very upset when she went to her room last night, despite my best efforts to reassure her. Since I heard her moving around until quite late through our adjoining wall, I assumed she had a difficult time finding rest. Hence the reason for my delay to rouse her this morning."

"This is not right," Borth muttered.

Placing his palm on the door panel, he input the emergency override and stepped into the room as the door slid open. His heart stilled, the breath leaving his lungs as he stared at the unslept-in bed still piled with the bags that she had brought back from the market.

He shook his head in denial, his eyes darting around the room and falling upon the datapad and ear transponders sitting beside the bed before roving over to the open closet. The black bag that she had when she arrived and all of her simple clothing from Earth were gone.

She had left… and taken nothing from them with her.

He turned and swallowed painfully as he watched Grish slowly walk over to the table, his large fingers awkwardly picking up the tiny transponders. The male blinked, the moisture rimming one eye falling away to roll down his cheek as he gathered them up with the datapad and held them to his chest.

She had left everything, leaving every trace of her time with them behind. The pain of loss suddenly stabbed deep within Borth, and he stumbled back until he sat heavily upon the bed, the soft clothing rustling at the movement. He could still scent traces of her on the bedding and on the clothes from when she tested their fit. Though the latter was far fainter, it didn't pain him any less.

"We have lost our mate," Grish rumbled sorrowfully.

Borth dropped his head, the weight of guilt and grief unbearable. He felt like he could not breathe, as if he were drowning under some force even greater than the grief he had felt when he realized that he would never be the same after he left Agraadax. Losing his leg had struck him a grievous injury—but losing Crystal would be the end of him. He would have nothing left without her.

His breath trembled as it heaved from him. His fist curled tight on his leg, and he shook his head violently, horns swinging through the air with fierce denial.

No! He would not lose her!

"We are not losing her," he repeated aloud to Grish, his voice booming in the small room.

His brother's head swung up, a hope brightening the dimness that had come to his eyes. Grish swallowed thickly and nodded in agreement as he clutched the mating gifts bestowed upon their female tightly to his chest.

"We will not," he agreed in a deep rolling bass. "But where do we even begin to search for her?"

"Bring up the security systems," Borth shot off rapidly. "We will see if there is any clue there."

Grish pulled the datapad away from his chest, and his hands moved over it, bringing up their domicile's systems. A confused frown suddenly pulled at the male's face, and he shook his head in bewilderment.

"There is nothing there at all for the span of an hour. She turned off all systems when she left so there would be no recordings of her departure."

Borth let out a weak laugh despite himself. "Clever female."

"Brother, there is one thing. She has left something for us," Grish said quietly, drawing Borth's attention.

The other lifted up the datapad, tilting it so that they both could see, and drew up the tiny flashing icon of a communication transmission. The datapads were not programmed to receive direct transmissions. They could only receive direct files from a comm docked to it. Seems she figured a way around that as well.

Touching a finger to the icon, a window opened. Crystal stared back at them, her eyes shadowed with exhaustion. Borth wanted to demand that she come home, but he knew this was only a recording from sometime earlier. A tiny, sad smile tugged at her lips before she pressed them in a tight line, blinking back tears. Her voice wavered as she spoke, and his chest tightened at the pain in her voice.

"Borth, Grish, by the time you receive this I'll be long gone. I've figured something out for myself. Maybe it's not where I wanted to be, but I can take some comfort in knowing I can do some good there. I didn't want to leave before I had a chance to tell you goodbye… and that I'm sorry. You were right that I came here to run away and hide. Even though I wanted to live out my own happily ever after, I had a backup plan in case Borth never came around. Grish—sorry you spent a crapton of credits on the intergalactic comm system. If I can ever repay it, I will. The Mate Index Distribution Program had discovered what I did some time ago, and this was my last shot. Even if there was a way to go back to Earth and escape the notice of the Calystii, I'd be in jail for a very long time."

Crystal glanced down and took a deep breath, her lip trembling. When she looked up again, tears ghosted down her cheeks, and she swiped her palms over her face. "I really wanted to be with you. I hope you believe that. I'm not entirely sure what I feel… I'm not good with people things and emotions, but I did want you. From the bottom of my heart. I wanted you both more than I wanted anything. I wish things could have been different."

A watery sigh escaped her as she dropped her head. She sat that way for a moment, deep in thought, before she lifted her head again, a tremulous smile on her face. "Anyway, this is it. I have obscured my departure as much as I can. I only hope it's enough that the Calystii won't disturb you much, and you'll be able to go back to your lives as soon as possible. You will both be with me, in my mind and heart."

A soft voice called in the distance and Crystal glanced over her shoulder.

"Yes, I'm coming!" She faced the screen again and offered an apologetic grin. "Time to go. Bye, boys," she said, pressing her fingers to her lips in a gesture of kissing as the recording ended.

Grish sighed, but Borth nudged him sharply in the side.

"Go back."

"How far?" Grish asked, his brow ridges raising with inquiry.

"To just before she turned. I want to you to isolate the voice of whoever is speaking. Can you do that?"

"I am not as good at this as our mate is," Grish muttered. "But I will try."

Again and again, they went over the segment as Grish worked

at drawing out the voice. Finally, they were able to hear it, though faint in the background.

"Come, we must go now, Crystal," a female called out.

Borth recognized that voice. He had known that the females were on pleasant terms and that Talimia had offered to teach their female how to cook, but Wanits tended to be isolated and not invite intrusion from other species. Why would she help Crystal?

Grish swung toward the door, leaving Borth to stumble after him in a clumsy attempt to catch up. "Nargis has much to answer for," the male growled impatiently.

For the first time in revolutions, Borth was of the same mind as his uthak brother.

CHAPTER 18

"Are you sure that this is the place you want to meet? A teahouse?" Talimia said as they walked through the dusty streets toward the one familiar sight that was actually welcoming in Crystal's memory.

"Yes, this is exactly the place," Crystal confirmed with a thin smile. "It's a safe place to hold a meeting, which is why I chose it. I commed the proprietress, Nikana, on our way over. She's expecting us."

The teahouse was quiet, the afternoon light spilling through the curtained windows near the front. Wisps of perfumed smoke rolled through the air as cups clinked softly. There weren't many patrons at that hour, the few who were present scattered throughout the dim interior, sipping silently at their cups or engaged in quiet conversations. No one paid attention to the entrance of a human and Wanit, and that was exactly how Crystal wanted it.

At the far end of the room, Nikana glanced up and met her eyes. The Morith nodded in greeting and swept out from behind a long counter painted a deep ruby hue. Her robes, belted to her body with a wide, ornately beaded belt, fluttered loosely around her ankles as she walked over. At her approach, her arms opened to loosely embrace Crystal, the Morith's warm hands clasping around her shoulders before releasing her. A light musky scent lingered after the female pulled away.

Although Crystal stiffened habitually out of surprise in response to the greeting, she smiled. While it wasn't normal among many human cultures to be so familiar with virtual strangers, she found the Morith female's natural friendliness to be as oddly charming as she remembered.

"Crystal, good to see you again. I am sad to hear that you are leaving our planet, but I am glad you chose my establishment for your meeting so that you might say a proper goodbye before you leave."

"Of course. I couldn't think of any place more suitable, and I wouldn't have dreamed of leaving without saying goodbye first. You were very kind to me when I arrived."

Nikana sighed with a sorrow that seemed a little exaggerated, but the regret in her eyes was genuine as she regarded Crystal sadly. "It is not often we receive females here. I was so certain that everything was going to work between you and that handsome Teril. Perhaps it might have encouraged more mate contracts. This place needs more females—more families." Straightening, she gave Crystal an understanding smile. "But these things happen. Come with me. I have the perfect table for you. When are you expecting to meet with your…ah, client?"

Crystal glanced at the empty corner that Nikana led them to and shrugged. "I'm not sure. He didn't give me a definite time for arrival. I may be waiting for some time, I'm afraid. I hope that won't be too inconvenient."

The Morith made a small rolling sound in her throat. "Not at all. The midweek is always slow. Take as much time as you need. I shall bring intimbar, and you tell me whatever else you might need."

"I don't have much in the way of credits," Crystal protested.

"Your bill is covered by the house today," Nikana insisted gently. "Just be sure to tell your lovely human friends about our planet. It is sometimes rowdy in the ports, and perhaps not much to do for some, but there is a good life to be had here."

Crystal smiled and nodded. She didn't have much in the way of friends anymore… well, none really, aside from Talimia, since she'd severed all contact with people she knew on Earth, but she agreed with Nikana's appraisal of Antari Minor. Although it lacked the cosmopolitan excitement of other worlds, she was happier there than she'd been anywhere else for a long time.

"I'll be sure to mention that it was a very good home while it lasted," she replied, doing her best to keep her heartache from her voice.

Nikana patted her arm and hurried away to attend to another patron flagging her down at another table with enthusiasm and maternal affection. Crystal chuckled under her breath. Obviously the Morith was very free with her affections as she elegantly sailed around the room.

Sitting on the nearest pillow, Crystal turned just enough so that she had a view of the door. Although she was confident that her contact was who he said he was, she wasn't going to immediately trust the word of a stranger, sight unseen. Nikana stopped minutes later with a tray and set two cups of intimbar on the table in front of them. Crystal nodded her appreciation, earning her a smile from the Morith before she was hurrying off again. Sighing, Crystal leaned back in her seat and sipped at her drink.

This was likely going to be a long wait.

At her side, Talimia glanced down at her comm and frowned.

"Something wrong?"

The Wanit shook her head, her lips pressing into a hard line. "Not wrong, but Nargis is fussing about having to evade your males. Apparently, they have deduced where you went and have arrived at our property."

Crystal's eyebrows rose. "Males? As in both of them?"

Wasn't Borth just bellowing at her only the evening before? Although she suspected that Grish might try to come after her to make sure she was okay, she hadn't anticipated Borth searching for her. The reverse hunt idea that Talimia had jumped onto was something that she'd gone along without commentary, but she had never expected it.

Talimia snickered and closed her comm. "Apparently so. Nargis is currently hiding. He says that Terils are notoriously difficult to keep secrets from so he figures that hiding is the better strategy, but he is warning us that our location may not be unknown for long and advises to conclude whatever business you have arranged as soon as possible if you do not want them to catch you too soon."

Crystal rubbed her temples. This wasn't what she had planned. She was trying to evade the Calystii and keep the Ugaar brothers safe. How the fuck was it helping them if they were intentionally trying to track her down? Moreover, did she even want to be found? The way her stupid heart soared at the announcement and the little thrill that currently ran through her would suggest yes, but her brain—the sensible one—was hitting the brakes hard.

She had an opportunity to do something that mattered with her life… Was she going to set that aside to go back to the farm with Borth and Grish after her heart had been trampled all over?

It wasn't that she didn't understand how it might have looked if the situation were reversed, but could she trust that they could move on, that she would be able to have a life with Borth and Grish?

Borth had never given her any promises before the trust between them soured. She couldn't see it happening now. The likelihood of being a family with them after everything that happened felt near impossible now. Even she had to admit that, if she were looking at it from an outside perspective, she would've declared it a stupid risk to take.

Her heart, that insisted on giving things a chance and see where they went—that longed for love and a happily ever after—was an idiot.

Licking her lips, Crystal adopted a nonchalant air and shrugged. There was a chance that they would decide not to follow her all the way to Intakfell, much less anywhere else. In any case, she hadn't even met with the Lorgor yet, so it was too soon to worry about anything.

Taking a sip of her intimbar, she settled more comfortably into her chair. There was absolutely no reason to even try to decide until she had more facts to work with.

CHAPTER 19

Grish narrowed his eyes on the Wanit male sitting on a tree branch high overhead. Nargis was clearly exhausted, his chest heaving in an attempt to regain control of his breathing. He was also clinging to the tree with a tight grip, no doubt from yet another tiny earthquake that shook the ground. It was stronger than the small tremors they had been having, so he could understand why it would alarm the male, given his precarious place in the tree.

That the male was avoiding them altogether told him all he needed to know.

Nargis knew exactly where their female was.

"Come down!" Borth bellowed, fists balled at his sides.

The Wanit had good reason not to come down from the tree. Smears of mud streaked down both Borth and Grish's flanks from the mad chase that Nargis had given them through the property. It was no wonder their tempers were frayed.

Grish had hoped for a reasonable discussion with the male. They had barely gotten out a greeting before the Wanit took off with surprising speed into his orchards. They had managed to corner him at last, but Grish knew that his brother's knee was likely protesting the activity, despite the brace supporting it. It was no doubt contributing to Borth's foul mood. In fact, he looked ready to outright kill the male.

"If I come down, you will only harm me!" Nargis called back.

"An accurate observation!" Borth shouted in return. "But if you force me to chop down this tree to remove you, I will definitely kill you and hide your body so well that even a team of excavators will not find it!"

Grish's brow ridges rose. His brother was angrier than he had surmised. He wasn't pleased with the male, but it not a good idea to murder one's neighbors, no matter how vexing they were.

Moving closer to the tree, he eyed the male. For a Wanit, he was remarkably calm in the face of their anger. Usually, the species didn't handle pressure well, not even males who were accustomed to long periods of aggressive pursuit by females who desired to mate them. Despite his hard grip on the tree, Nargis was composed as he returned his stare.

"Come down, Nargis," Grish sighed. "There's no reason for us to be at odds with each other. I do not even understand why you ran. We have always assisted each other in the past and have both benefitted from our friendship."

"Even if you did betray us," Borth grumbled.

"I did not betray anyone! You would not understand. It is the law of the hunt," the testy male growled back.

Grish paused, one large hand coming down on his brother's shoulder to calm him. Peering through the branches, he met the other male's eyes. "What do you mean, the law of the hunt?"

"I should not say," Nargis muttered. "But if I do not say, then you will not know the rules."

"Yes, tell us the rules," Grish called out.

A suspicious look flooded the Wanit's features as he watched Borth. "You swear that you will not harm me or my mate?"

"We swear it," Grish answered at once.

"Not you. You will swear easily. Borth must swear."

At his brother's hesitation, Grish shot him a menacing look. He had tolerated much ill-tempered behavior over the revolutions, had even attempted to soothe Crystal's worries and stall her until he could calm him—but enough was enough. He wasn't going to risk any further when it came to their female.

"Borth," he growled.

"Yes, I swear," Borth capitulated with a grimace.

The Wanit nodded and dropped down with a graceful ease from the tree. Brushing his hands on his pants, he eyed the pair of them, his lips tightening.

"First let me say this without fear of recompense: you are an idiot. I say this because only an idiot will have to go through the trials of being the hunter."

Grish frowned in confusion. "I thought the females hunted the males in your species."

"Yes," Nargis agreed. "Unless the male is an idiot. Then the female who hunted and worked to capture his affection will be the prey, and he will not have an easy hunt. He must prove himself again and show he's strong enough, capable enough, and smart enough to regain her affections. Not an easy thing. For this reason, you are an idiot. Doubly so because my female, the keenest of huntresses, is assisting your female. It is the right and duty of friends and sisters to do so for each other in our culture."

"She took her somewhere," Borth surmised.

Nargis grimaced. "There is more than that, I am afraid. She allowed her access to our intergalactic comm system. From what information I was able to gather, your female arranged to meet for an opportunity of employment and transport from our world... They are meeting today."

Borth stalked forward and likely would have snatched the male up in his huge hands, but Grish grabbed his brother's arm, pulling the male up short. The frustrated growl was understandable, but Grish ignored the tempest of emotions that washed over him and focused on the Wanit before them. The haze of despair, fear, and anger toward any male that would even dare approach their mate and take her away continued to linger on the periphery of his mind, but it was at least manageable, for the time being.

"Where?"

A mutinous look appeared on the male's face. "I am certain telling you outright is against the laws of the hunt. Wouldn't be much of a hunt if you were provided everything and she were just handed over to you."

"Blessed gods, save me from unreasonable rules and regulations," Borth muttered. "I was certain that we left that life behind with our retirement from the Fleet!" Running his hand over his face, he stilled and regarded the male with a cool calm that Grish hadn't seen in his brother since their days of battling side by side. The sight of it elated him. "Can you answer yes or no so that we may gather clues?"

The Wanit paused, a speculative look in his eye as he thought it over. "Yes, I believe there is no law against that."

"Good… Did she leave here at an early hour in the company of your mate?"

"Yes, the sun had just risen."

"So just after she sent that message," Grish muttered to his brother.

Borth nodded as he jerked free from Grish's hold only to pace in front of the male, his large frame shadowing the smaller male. Although he did not attack, Grish bit back a smile at the subtle dominance his brother was exuding as he posed his queries.

"Did they take one of your land vessels to town?"

"No, the rover is stationed in the docking unit on our home."

"A flyer then. She went far with our female… to Intakfell perhaps? If she is traveling for a distance, the port would be the most obvious destination." The last was said more in aside to Grish, and he nodded in agreement with his brother.

"Yes," the male sighed with an obvious measure of relief. "They would have arrived just a short time ago."

"Do you know where she is meeting her contact?"

Nargis shook his head. "I did not hear that information. All I know was that it was a place she considered a safe spot within the port city. I think she knew someone there."

Borth snarled out his frustration and increased his pacing, one hand tugging at his horn in frustration. "What had she said of Intakfell… Does she know anyone?" he muttered to himself.

Grish frowned. Crystal had only been to Intakfell once, when she waited for him to pick her up. She had not seemed comfortable and familiar with her surroundings when they met. In fact, just the opposite. If it weren't for the kindly watchful eye of Nikana and the heavily enforced peaceful sanctuary that the teahouse provided, there was little doubt in his mind that she would have been absolutely terrified by the time he arrived to collect her.

He froze, his mind quieting in surprise.

"Brother, I know where she is," he said, his voice unnaturally loud in the silence that had fallen.

Borth spun around to face him, his eyes widening. Only the slightest limp was evident as he hurried over to Grish, something painfully too much like hope brightening his expression.

"*Where?*"

The word was spoken quietly but with such heartfelt intensity that Grish smiled, the tension easing from him. Their mate was safe for the time being, and Borth was obviously mellowing, his thoughts entirely on their female rather than rankling with unspent aggression toward an unknown male.

"The teahouse," Grish announced with a pleased grin. "I was delayed in meeting her and the Itashvanda had to continue on their route, and so they had her wait for me at the teahouse. Nikana kept an eye on her."

"What will you do if the male contests your claim on her?" the Wanit asked curiously, following after them as they turned to stalk out of the orchard. "Many species are lacking in females. To have one as skilled as herself would be considered a boon to many who might seek to use her abilities."

A hard smile curled Borth's mouth. "Then we will have to convince him otherwise."

"And convince our female that we are the better choice," Grish added.

Borth inclined his head in agreement, his expression sobering.

"Not a very sound strategy," Nargis muttered. "Do huntresses pursue with such little planning? It would seem foolhardy at best."

"I have to trust that our female is receptive. The heart is not logical. If she still holds some affection for us, I must trust that it is all we will require," Borth replied as he increased his pace.

"And if that does not work?" Nargis panted as he struggled to keep up.

Grish turned to grin at the male. "Then we go where she goes."

"The farm—all of this—it means nothing without her. If I must, I will have my entire leg refashioned so I can move fast enough to chase across the sectors."

Nargis stumbled to a stop, his mouth gaping in horror. "You would leave your farm? But this is all you have. You put everything into your farm—you have said so yourselves. You would have nothing without it."

"Wrong," Borth snarled. "I have had nothing before, and the farm did not provide me with anything other than simple comforts met. With her, I stand a chance of having everything, regardless of where we are."

Borth glanced back at Grish, and they exchanged a long look as he raised a brow ridge in silent inquiry of whether Grish would contest his statement. There was nothing to contest. What they had on their farm could easily be taken away and replaced, as the earthquake proved.

Their female was necessary for both of their happiness.

As Grish grinned in agreement, Borth's shoulders visibly relaxed, and an old, comfortable solidarity clicked into place between them once more. They were uthak brothers, their destinies entwined. All they were missing now was their mate, the final link to complete them.

They had found her after many revolutions.

And now they would retrieve her for the final time.

CHAPTER 20

The Lorgor who entered the teahouse was tall, but not quite as tall nor as muscular as most Lorgor that Crystal had seen before. Instead, there was a fluid gracefulness to the alien as he strode in that caught her attention. Otherwise, he looked very much like any other member of the species, the delicate teal scales shimmering under the light from the sinking sun. As she watched him, a small ruby webbed crest on his head flattened before snapping up again as his eyes met hers.

Crystal kept her expression neutral as the male approached with a crisp, fast stride, unwilling to make any snap decisions. His bearing appeared arrogant, as one perhaps accustomed to being in command positions, but there was an undeniable discipline to every movement that she couldn't help but admire. Everything about the Lorgor was effective and efficient. Not a single move was wasted. Even the clothing he wore was simple and well fitted.

In contrast to the Lorgor headed toward her, Crystal felt awkward and underqualified. What was she doing? She was no resistance fighter. She did simple jobs to tighten security or breach it… Her last job was programing a damn watering system. Her breath burst out of her in a panicked rasp, and her fingers tightened on her leggings.

Get ahold of yourself! This was only an interview. There was no reason to be anything but open to whatever he had to say and then wait and see from there. No one was going to make a decision that day. Thanks to Talimia, she had enough credits available to secure lodgings for the night.

By measures, she managed to calm herself before the Lorgor arrived at her table. His eyes swept over Talimia before narrowing on Crystal.

"A human?" the melodic voice demanded in confusion. "I do not understand. I am to meet a qualified coder by name of…" He squinted at his comm, and Crystal's outrage at being dismissed for her race turned to sympathy as the silence stretched on.

"Crystal Rivers," she filled in stiffly. "That would be me." She stabbed her thumb toward her breast. "And you are?"

The Lorgor eyed her blankly for a long. Finally, he shrugged in a manner that she recognized all too well as the *"not my prob-lem"* expression before settling himself on the pillow opposite hers. He leaned forward and dropped his voice as he spoke.

"I am Danit Telmafursenet, daughter of the first general of the resistance, and your arranged contact."

"But Lorgor females never go offplanet!" Talimia exclaimed from her side.

Danit's violet eyes slid over to the Wanit, and the Lorgor frowned. "And this is a friend of yours?"

"Yes," Crystal replied. "Is there a problem with that?"

Anyone who expected her to meet alone would have to say their farewells to her well-rounded ass. She needed a job, but she wasn't going to set herself up to have something awful happen to her by being stupid.

She wasn't going to trust this Lorgor further than she could throw her.

The female's crest snapped again—the only sign of her impatience—before she settled back onto her pillow.

"It is of no consequence," she answered, tone flat.

With that, the interview began. Danit asked her dozens of nuanced questions and produced a datapad with numerous scenarios programmed into it for her to solve. Crystal wasn't sure exactly how long she was at it, but long enough that the sun gave off only the faintest remaining rays of light and sank behind the mountains as she finished.

By that time, a begrudging respect filled the other female's eyes as she looked over her work. Crystal was only distantly aware of the doors opening as customers filed in and out of the teahouse. They were of no concern. From the corner of her eye, she could see Nikana watching the traffic from her place behind the counter.

"You are good. That much is apparent. I see that my brother chose well. Very well, Crystal Rivers. I am hereby authorized to offer you immediate transport to Lorgoon. Upon arrival, you will be…"

"Not going anywhere," a deep voice growled.

Crystal's head shot up, her eyes widening as they met Borth's hard gaze.

The Lorgor's crest snapped up, and the female hissed. "I suggest that you leave the way you came. Our business does not concern you."

Borth's expression morphed into a fierce glower, his large frame shifting toward Danit as he bent just enough to meet her eyes.

"Our *mate* is our business," he growled as Grish stepped up behind him, his expression unreadable as he stared down the Lorgor.

Danit faltered, and then she looked at Crystal. "Your mates? You did not say that you were mated to Terils. This changes everything," she said.

"What do you mean?" Crystal asked.

Although she directed the question to Danit, it applied to everyone. To the Ugaar brothers who publicly claimed her and to the Lorgor whose face now lit up with excitement as she whispered in a low voice into her comm. As if the Terils were no longer any kind of threat, the female stood and moved away from the table. Crystal watched her leave with confusion before glancing back toward the males hovering over her.

Mate? Changed everything? What the fuck was going on?

As the Lorgor wandered farther away, the Terils closed in, their faces set with stony resolve as they hemmed her in. Talimia at her side spat angrily, distracting Crystal from the looming males.

"This is *not* how the hunt is done!" she snarled. "You do not get to demand. You prove yourself. You win her by your efforts."

"And we shall," Borth countered firmly. "By working together, we were able to track her to your domicile. By trapping your mate, we were able to deduce her location despite his stubborn uncooperativeness. We traveled here faster than what it is advisable in our flyer to assure ourselves that she would not escape before our arrival. We willingly surrender everything we have to hold her once more. And should she continue running, we will continue to follow her throughout the sectors."

The last was bit out so sternly that Crystal could only gape at him while a pleased smile spread on the Wanit female's face. Talimia didn't say anything more. She gave Crystal an approving nod and sat back down, letting her hash things out alone from there.

Crystal shook her head in disbelief. "You can't leave your farm for me! Are you crazy? Only a day ago you didn't even want me and were ready to send me back to Earth to preserve what peace and life you have. What you're suggesting doesn't even make sense."

Borth shifted closer to her, sighing as Grish nudged him with his elbow.

"I know I do not deserve it, but I am asking your forgiveness. You have made me happier than I have any right to be… even when you were tormenting me and not giving me any peace." His lips tilted slightly at that before falling solemnly once more. "I knew I made a mistake, that my fear had conquered me. I knew before the night was out and hastened to your room to apologize in the early hours of the morning. Despite the anger and paranoia I had shown in that moment, I know you would never be so cruel as I had accused you. You have never shown me anything less than kindness, affection, and patience when you were not required or expected to. My brother Grish tolerates me, perhaps more than he should, but what you gave me in the time you have been with us has been a gift."

Swallowing past the lump that had formed in her throat, she blinked the away the tears brimming her eyes. "So what exactly are you saying here?"

He stepped closer so that she was nearly touching him before dropping to his knees. She shot to her feet and grabbed at him in dismay, watching the pain flash over his features from the weight he suddenly put on his knee.

"Borth, don't…"

"You will allow me this," he grunted. "I must beg the forgiveness of the female who brings the only joy into my life that I have known in many revolutions." A shudder racked his large frame as he leaned his head forward and brushed his ganthli against her belly. "I do not deserve forgiveness for my unkindness, but I beg for it. I beg for the privilege to worship you and shower you with adoration for the rest of my days."

She was at a loss for words, startled when Grish also dropped down to his knees at her other side, his head bowing forward as well.

"Forgive your males who have erred and accept that we have proven the strength of our love for you," he rumbled. When he lifted his head, his beautiful amber eyes were red-rimmed with tears. His hands went to a pouch, and he gently removed the ear transponders and datapad. "I do not want to walk the rest of my days with nothing but the memory of you by our side. I want my female back. I want our family whole."

She pressed her lips together at his earnest gaze, trying not to cry, trying to think logically and not to be swept away by her heart.

"And what if you do it again? What if you change your mind and remove me from your home? I can't go through this all again. I have a chance to do something worthwhile… to hit back at the Calystii who've been tormenting me for years. Do I give that up all in the hope that you won't change your mind?"

Borth shook his head, a small smile curling his lips. "It would be impossible to make you leave."

His words not only surprised her but Grish as well, who glanced over at his brother in confusion. His smile widened, and for a moment, she was certain that she was seeing the Borth that Grish had spoken of—the male had been before his injury. The male she caught only fleeting glimpses of.

His fingers fumbled on his comm for a moment before hers blinked with a received transmission. He gestured to it.

"Open it."

Her fingers trembling anxiously, she opened the message and her breath caught in her throat. This was… impossible. She glanced up at him, her eyes searching his face.

"Is this what I think it is?"

"I hope so, or I did something incorrect," he chuckled. "On

our way here, I realized that the only thing that could really show you just how much you are a part of us—a part of our family—would be by a visible gesture. Something that would be your right as our mate. I know I made excuses that I could not promise anything, and that I needed time. That is what I told myself and you. I was not certain if you would want this," he gestured to himself, "when you saw me riddled with pain in the worst months of the year."

"I wouldn't have left you," she whispered. "I know you have problems because of your leg. You lost it on Agraadax, right?"

He nodded. "It is hard, from our background that places all praise upon our strength as males, to feel worthy, broken as I am. I deal with the torment placed on my knee because I cannot bear losing more of my flesh, to have the entire leg replaced with something that would work better and not pain me. I do not feel worthy of you… That is why it was so easy to push you away. It is easier than having you eventually leave me when you tire of my imperfections and my pain."

Her lips parted. "I wouldn't have left you, you idiot. I would have dragged your sorry ass to a medic and had that damn surgery. What the fuck were you thinking? You didn't replace it with something you needed out of fucking pride? Gods, I could murder you right now! That's it! When we get home, you're going to set up an appointment, and I am going to personally…"

His laughter cut her off, and his large hand covered hers, his amber-red eyes shining with emotion. "I knew you were just the female I needed… and Grish knew it… I just needed to let myself see it. And now that I have, I commed the land management offices and had your name officially added to our property. We are yours, if you will have us, just as our land is now yours. And if you decide to go with the Lorgor, then we will arrange for a caretaker, I will get my leg taken care of, and we will follow you."

"You would really do that for me?"

Both males nodded solemnly, their warm eyes resting on her, allowing her to bask in the love in those bright depths.

"We know that the Calystii need to be dealt with, and outside of hunting down your Robby, we understand if you would feel safer among the rebellion until you are certain. Just be aware that no matter where we are, we will always guard you and care for you," Grish murmured. "Our farm can wait for us."

"I may have a more satisfactory solution," a deep voice broke in as a large Lorgor approached, accompanied by Danit. His eyes raked over them before settling on Crystal, the corners of his mouth rising as he ignored the territorial growl of her males.

"What sort of solution?" she asked cautiously.

The male's smile widened. "It happens that my sister realized she was speaking to a female we have been searching for over many revolutions. We only recently intercepted word that you were on this planet, mated to a pair of Terils, but the communication was incomplete and did not provide us with any information regarding your name or where on Antari Minor you were located. Danit did not realize your identity since we were lacking more precise information and—forgive me—but you humans all look alike to us. Finding you has done more for us than you can know."

"But I don't have anything," Crystal said helplessly.

"And the Calystii are stubbornly ignoring that fact," the male agreed pleasantly.

"And what is this solution you speak of?" Borth demanded as he moved forward, placing the solid muscle of his body between her and the Lorgor.

"Nothing that demands any action at this moment," the male assured him. "Take your mate home and solidify your claim. Leave the details to the resistance. We will contact you when it is time."

Nostrils flaring, hot breath blew out with unmistakable anger as Borth met the Lorgor's eyes.

"Do not even consider putting my mate in danger or in any fashion using her as bait. I have already been forced to threaten death on my neighbor—and I liked him enough to offer to bury him. Do not cross me when it comes to my female, because I will not be so gracious with you."

Grish growled in agreement as he slid forward as well until Crystal was walled in behind an enormous barrier of muscle.

"We may be retired, but we are still Fleet. We know more ways to break a male than anyone in your resistance or the Calystii Army has ever imagined," Grish added in a threatening tone she had never even heard come from the typically jubilant, sweet male.

"Understood," the Lorgor said with clear interest in his voice. "Yes, I do think that this will be quite beneficial. Until we speak again," he said.

Crystal managed to elbow between her males just in time to see the retreating forms of the Lorgors as they exited the teahouse. Glancing up between the Ugaar brothers, she grinned cheerfully.

"So... what now?"

Borth glanced down at her, one brow ridge rising. "Now we go home."

Squeezing between them, she wrestled her way out into the open room and spun around, still grinning. "That sounds great and all, since I *am* co-owner, but you know... I just can't make any promises about this whole business yet."

Borth growled, stalking forward as Talimia's peals of laughter filled the room. Crystal kept smiling up at the surly male as he scooped her up and lifted her until she dangled from his hands like a helpless kitten. He brought her eye to eye with him.

"Very well," he rumbled. "And I will continue my pursuit until you agree… for as long as it takes."

"Well, those *are* the rules of the hunt," she quipped cheerfully.

CHAPTER 21

They did not wait to arrive back at their farm to renew their connection to their mate. Borth did not remember how exactly they arrived at their overnight lodging, nor did he recall any details about the Mintigi clerk who coded their room access. His entire attention was on his mate.

Unless someone attempted to come between them or acted in a way that posed a threat that triggered his lethal attention to them, Borth was consumed with absolute need for their female. Running along that need was the frustration that they could not claim their female as their mate... Not yet, not until she invited it.

Part of him was willing to bind her to him anyway and face the consequences afterward. He was not going to do that—but it tempted him, especially with the way her soft hands skimmed over his scales and her lips brushed against his chest as they stood in the lift waiting to arrive on the level their room was on. Her body was pressed against his intimately, his cock jutting into the soft flesh just above her belly due to their size difference and Grish behind her. She was between them, her hands roaming over both of them eagerly. It was at once the most wondrous and torturous feeling. He pressed back against her, just as demanding as he leaned down to nip her neck.

She seized his horn suddenly, and a low growl echoed from the chambers of his ganthli in response. His fingers bit into her hips as she giggled at his unrestrained reaction, happiness bursting through him. In vengeance, he stroked his tongue over a sensitive spot on her throat until she groaned and twitched against him. Grish chuckled, his large hands massaging her breasts and plucking gently on her nipples through the long shirt she wore.

The sweet scent of her arousal filled the lift with every touch, mingling his and Grish's pheromones. That combined smell was intoxicating, making his cock ache against his pants. The desire to just peel her pants down and take her with her small, soft body held up against Grish called to him.

Not there. He was not going to join with her in the lift.

He met Grish's gaze, and his brother's lips twitched in amusement, no doubt guessing at his impatience. He wondered if the male guessed at just how hard the temptation was driving him to strike his claim. Even before Agraadax, Borth had not been the most patient of males. Now with the female he desired to mate under his hands, the threat to his control was even more challenging.

When the door to the lift slid open, it wasn't a moment too soon for him. With Crystal still pressed up against him, it took little effort to lift her high into his arms and carry her into the corridor. Her laughter was long, loud and sweet. It startled a pair of Orwols coming from their room, their long ears snapping toward her, but they soon relaxed and shared a smile before continuing to the lift, leaving Grish and Borth plenty of space to maneuver their female into their room. Grish stepped forward just enough to place his palm against the locking panel before the door opened to admit them.

With the door open, Borth charged forward, his shoulder

slamming into a nearby wall. Crystal had chosen to nip him at the base of the neck playfully just as they entered, and he had misjudged its distance. The loud crack of his arm against the wall had her shooting him an apologetic look, but he did not mind. He truthfully barely even felt it. Terils were built sturdy and from their youth were well accustomed to slamming against both inanimate and animate things—most especially each other as they trained or asserted dominance. The wall barely registered on his good side after a lifetime of such activity.

Instead, he grinned as Grish joined them, the male divesting himself of his clothes in the process. Their mate caught once more between them, they moved through the room awkwardly toward the bed, thumping several more times against walls and furnishings in their eager desire. In the process, they stripped her small body of clothing before Borth transferred her to Grish's embrace so he too could undress.

When they finally got Crystal onto the bed, low rumbles of pleasure and happiness filled the room, joined by her soft gasps and sighs as hands caressed and mouths tasted. Borth's eyes threatened to cross when her fingers closed tightly around his cock. Crystal's pleased murmur at his reaction filled his ears. Squirming, her body slid down him until her mouth was aligned with his cock. The touch of her tongue on his straining, aching sex sent sparks shooting through his veins, thighs trembling as he battled against his rapidly rising release.

Not yet...

He hissed an oath as she sucked harder, a soft grunt coming from her around his cock as Grish buried himself deep within her from behind, rocking her with the force of his thrust. Although her mouth was barely large enough to take the first inch beyond his head, Borth canted his hips helplessly as her tongue traced the veins that rose beneath the scales, the hot suction drawing up a wave of pleasure so fierce that he nearly shook with it.

Or perhaps it was more than just his physical response to her that he was shaking with. Her every touch affected him not only bodily, but soothing his heart as well. He would never be whole or perfect in the eyes of his people, but with her, he did not have to be. He was more than enough just as he was, and she both desired and loved him. He could feel the acceptance as her fingers trailed gently over where his prosthetic met his flesh, as accepting of it as if his leg were still whole. Gods knew that his love for her swept through him with such strength that for a moment he couldn't separate the two pleasures he was experiencing at once.

Groaning, he shifted his hips away, pulling his cock from her mouth with a wet pop. Grish's pace increased as Borth braced her in his arms, his hips slamming against her bottom. Crystal's mouth fell open, her breath coming out in delicate, lusty pants, her muscles quivering. She ground back, angling her body a bit more so that Grish's sack struck her clit with a bit more force as he rutted against her.

She was beautiful. The freckles that had appeared on her skin in the early days on their farm had long since smoothed out into a beautiful light bronze, her dark eyes shining. Borth watched her every expression as she climaxed, her hips jerking in Grish's grasp, his own hips thumping out a harder, faster rhythm until a bellow shook him as he too found his release. The sight of their mutual desire spurred on Borth's own arousal so he was more than ready when it was his turn. With their female currently not fertile, they could stretch out their pleasure, and he and his brother were greedy for it.

With a low growl as Grish pulled himself free of their female's glorious body, they shifted her around until she was stretched over Borth. Notching the head of his cock at her sopping entrance, Borth pushed home in one long, firm thrust, groaning at the sensation of her channel griping his flesh. His tail stiffened at the sensation. He had no doubt that if he were able to rise comfortably to his knees like Grish, his tail would have stood straight from his body as his brother's had.

Their tails were flexible enough, like those of the Edoka, Agraak, and a number of other species. They could not wind them around their mates and hold her to them. They were too club-like in their sharp swing, but as they stiffened in the midst of pleasure, a Teril was guaranteed to be able to instinctively warn or fight off anyone who dared to approach. Trapped beneath him, his tail was unable to rise like it wanted to, but lust flamed through him at the sultry look their female gave him, and that alone was well worth it.

Sinuously, she moved over him, her hips rolling exotically as he lifted and lowered her upon him. Although his fingers grasped her thighs, he gave over control to her and watched through hooded eyes as her body danced over his, every erotic movement caressing him in a new way, heightening his pleasure while she looked down at him, a soft smile tipping her lips as her expression filled with love.

She owned him in that moment, the dark curtain of her hair brushing over him when she leaned down to brush kisses against him as she claimed him as hers.

Mating or not, he was hers in every way.

Then her expression changed, her full lips falling open in soft pants as she came down on him harder and faster, sparking the sharp crescendo of his own lust, tightening his sack. A shiver ran over her skin as he felt her sex ripple around him, drawing him deeper as it convulsed around him with her release. Her soft cry was followed shortly by his roar as his seed shot out in streams and he buried himself deep within her.

His body slowly coming down from ecstasy, he smiled as Grish leaned forward to nuzzle the back of her neck. He gathered her in his arms and gently pulled out, his cock slowly softening from where it was wedged within her. The slurping sound of their bodies parting was enticing, but Borth rolled to his side as Crystal was settled between them. With her body replete and softened in a post-coital glow, she was the most beautiful and most perfect thing he had ever seen.

"However long you need," he murmured. "You have my heart, forever."

"And mine," Grish rumbled.

"I love you guys too," she whispered softly.

She was not yet ready to commit to be their mate, but those words swept through him with a wave of warmth. For now, hearing the words—knowing without a doubt that they had her love—it was enough.

CHAPTER 22

The weather was cooling rapidly, and everyone was working harder to harvest the rest of the crops. Even Crystal, who didn't know shit about harvesting, was out in the field with her guys, cutting down agrim to feed into the processor.

The grain had finally finished ripening, and now they were rushing to cut it and prepare it to be sold. Although a portion would be kept in an on-property silo to be sold at market, most of it was going to intergalactic distribution collectors, who were due to arrive any day. With the tremors stronger and more frequent, there was a noticeable anxiety in the air as they rushed to pull the harvest in.

It was grueling work. At the end of each day, she was left too achy and tired to do more than fall into bed with exhaustion. Muscles she hadn't been fully aware of possessing hurt. Even Grish seemed worn down. And Borth... It killed her every time she saw how much pain he was in by the end of the day.

She had tried to talk him into leaving Antari Minor on a trade vessel to get his surgery, but he refused. It was too important to harvest on time. More work than what Grish could accomplish even with her aid. His promise that he would get it taken care of once the harvest was complete was the only thing that kept her from losing it.

Despite his pain, he eagerly gathered her into his arms in the large bed that all three of them now shared. The steady, rhythmic beat of his heart against her ear every night as Grish curled protectively behind her had replaced the marathon sex they enjoyed the first weeks after returning home from Intakfell as her males attempted to convince her to accept their mate bond. She missed it, and despite her exhaustion, she longed for when she could enjoy being stretched out between them, sharing pleasure and love once more with them. To mate them. Still, being held between them gave her another sort of satisfaction that had her rising with a smile on her lips every morning.

Crystal groaned, her hands on the small of her back as she stretched, her cheeks flushed from the thought of mating. The securely bound bale of straw sat in front of her until Borth picked it up and tossed it, like it weighed nothing, into the back of a long transportation vehicle. Glancing over at Grish, she caught the way his eyes lingered on her breasts as he sealed a grain collector and rolled it off to the side. Replacing it with another large empty container, he winked at her flirtatiously.

"You look tired, *katna*. Why not go inside and find something cool to drink and rest? We are nearly done here."

Letting out a long sigh, she looked over the field, an odd sense of pride filling her. It had been hard work, but finally the fields of grain were threshed, the straw baled to be sold as animal bedding, and the grain stored for transportation offworld. They had done it.

"When is the collector arriving?" she asked.

"Two, three hours perhaps. Before nightfall. We finished just in time. The collectors do not like to be kept waiting," he explained with a chuckle.

"Uh-huh. Speaking from experience there, are you, handsome?"

"Perhaps a time or two," he agreed.

"I suppose we have time to have a cool drink and get some rest. Should I bring something outside?"

That was another thing that had happened that kept her busy. Talimia hadn't wasted time in beginning her cooking lessons and had been a hard taskmaster even when Crystal was nearly falling down with exhaustion. But as the Wanit had explained, a hard day of harvesting didn't mean that one's other responsibilities were over, and hard work needed to be fueled with filling food. With the approach of evening, however, something light and cool would be far more welcome and appropriate now that their work was complete.

"That would be welcome," Borth said as he sidled up next to her, stealing a kiss as Grish watched in amusement. "I think the collector is also bringing a special order Grish had rushed through for you."

Crystal's eyebrows rose. "An order for me?"

The males nodded, but didn't offer any explanation as they waved her off while they finished loading the transporter and storing the grain canisters. Pinching her lips together against a smile at their secretiveness, Crystal returned to the house and begin to prepare a pitcher of chilled saprili juice and sandwiches, made with cuts of leftover meat and sliced vegetables, for their evening meals.

With the pitcher and platter prepared, she moved everything out onto the table outside that Borth had built at her request as her males came in from the field. Their grateful smiles were warm as they each went in to wash their hands and strip off their leather coverings before joining her once more outside, where the dust and dirt from their work wouldn't further dirty the kitchen.

They had just finished their meal and settled to share some spice gifted to them by Talimia when a large shuttle dropped down through the atmosphere to settle at the nearest edge of their fields. The markings on its side weren't ones that she was familiar with, except for the bold insignia that marked it as property of the Intergalactic Council, the regulating force behind the grain distribution from private farmers. Those who worked under the Megaraisi Corporation turned their goods over to corporate representatives.

Crystal was glad that Borth and Grish hadn't let the corporation buy them out. It saved her from having to deal with any other unpleasant Calystii.

Instead, the male who left the shuttle and approached was a familiar species. The Teril male was about the same size as her mates, though perhaps a bit more polished in appearance in his pressed uniform. Hustling out behind him were other males from various species who immediately got to work loading the large grain canisters into the cargo bay of the shuttle. The Teril, however, strode purposely toward their house, but jerked to a halt in surprise at the sight of her between her mates.

"Borth, Grish," he greeted with an acknowledging sweep of his ganthli, his horns—*shorter than Borth's fine horns*, she thought with pride in response to the way the male looked at Borth's leg with a curled lip—arching through the air gracefully. "I was not aware you had taken a mate. A human, I see," he said, his lips quirking.

Crystal's brow dropped into a scowl. Was he mocking them for being mated to her? She had gotten the impression that many Terils were pretty snobby, especially as it would have been impossible for them to mate among their species due to Borth's injury—but this really took the cake. What was worse was that she could see her mates' expressions darkening in twin glares.

Clearly there was no love lost between them. And this was the guy they had to deal with every year? No wonder Grish was unrepentant about having to make him wait on occasion. Forcing her expression to relax, she smirked up at the asshole.

"They sure did," she said in a breezy voice. "I snagged them myself. I've never seen more powerful males in my life. These guys are obviously tough as nails, and hardworking farmers with their own land. Strong, dependable males are like catnip to human women, you know. I consider myself the luckiest woman alive to have them as my mates. We humans are sex fiends too, so color me lucky that your species comes in pairs! Maybe if you're lucky too, you'll be able to attract your own female. I mean, I guess you must have something going for you..."

She let her voice drop off speculatively, fighting back her grin as the male flushed with anger.

"Clearly your female is not aware of who I am," he bit out, his body rigid with temper.

"The collection guy? I figure that's kind of like the garbage guy, but instead of carting away junk you come fetch our grain so it can be distributed where needed. Don't worry. It's a perfectly good occupation. Don't let anyone tell you otherwise," she soothed as in her head, she laughed maniacally at the evidence of his mounting anger.

"Salk, leave our mate be. You have come to transfer our credits of purchase, I believe," Grish interrupted, drawing the male's attention back to him.

Crystal didn't know if the look on Salk's face could get any sourer as he reluctantly nodded and checked his comm. In the distance, she could see that all the canisters were gone, and the workers absent. No doubt they were sending over the final tallies.

"It appears that your harvest exceeded even last year. I am obligated to give one thousand, five hundred credits per canister. Transfer pending immediately."

Grish smiled and stretched out his comm, touching it to Salk's to initiate the transfer of credits. He appeared pleased, but not surprised. Crystal was too busy trying to add it all together, her eyes widening. Granted, each grain canister was nearly as big as she was tall and three times as round. Filled with grain, they were so heavy than only her males could budge them. There had been hundreds of canisters!

"As always, a great pleasure to do business with you, collector," Grish said pleasantly. "I hope all is well with your uthak and bonded mate."

The male bristled, his mouth falling further into an unpleasant scowl. "They are fine," he said roughly. "Imal finds various things to busy himself with as he watches over Minda. Last I heard, they were going into the greater city to attend the shops… again," he muttered as he pressed a few buttons on his comm, concluding the transaction.

Straightening, he glanced down at them, once again all business, when the ground suddenly shifted, heaving them all to the ground. The sturdy table held, but the chairs toppled over. Crystal could hear things falling in the house, even from outside. She thanked the gods that Borth had modified the storage units in the kitchen to place autolocks on them so they wouldn't lose more dishes. At least there wouldn't be that hell of a mess to clean.

Salk pushed himself to his feet and glanced back at the shuttle worriedly. "I believe that concludes everything," he said hastily as he brushed himself off. "We will be on our way then. I do not want to linger in the event that the rumors I have heard bear truth."

"Rumors?" Crystal asked, her brow furrowing as she glanced at her mates helping her up.

At first, she thought they were just as in the dark as she was until she saw the pensive pinch of their faces as they glanced at the mountain just beyond their farm.

"There is no way of knowing," Borth grumbled. "But we remain alert and ready to evacuate if needed. Until then, we will continue to maintain our farm."

"Wait, evacuate? What are you talking about?" Crystal asked, her body tensing as a sense of pending misfortune, one huge cosmic joke waiting to flatten her, loomed overhead.

Salk smiled tightly and gestured to her. "It seems your mate is ill-informed and not quite as willing to risk her wellbeing for a mere stretch of land. It is admirable that you have worked so hard —and so tirelessly—to get your crops in with an obvious threat so nearby."

"There is no way to accurately predict what will happen. Some planets have managed to do some accurate guesswork, but on Antari Minor it is still questionable that anything will come of it. It is a rarity on this planet," Borth gritted out from between his teeth.

"What are we talking about here?" Crystal hissed.

Salk raised a brow ridge at her tone. She knew that humans weren't exactly respected, their worth often calculated only by their ability to breed with aliens. That much she had discovered before she even joined the Mate Index Distribution Program. But to see it staring her in the face with the haughty way he looked down his nose at her, nostrils flaring as if incensed that she dared to raise her voice…

Well, fuck him!

"A volcano," he said, his voice cool of feeling as he dropped those two words on her.

Crystal blanched and stumbled back.

A fucking volcano?

Her eyes shot to the same mountains the males had been looking toward, the one that she frequently caught Grish and Borth looking at since she'd been with them.

They had suspected all that time.

"We are scanning alerts every day," Borth assured her quietly. "This is our home, but we will take no chances, I promise you. If the evacuation order comes, we will leave. We have amassed enough credits from the harvest to start over elsewhere if the worst happens. We are not going to be reckless in this."

"And what of the gorthals?" she asked.

There wasn't room in their flyer or the land cruiser for the animals, and she couldn't bear the idea of anything happening to Morosh—the name fitting for the flashy animal whose name meant gold in Mintigi.

Grish brushed his knuckles against her cheek. "We load them onto the load transporter and take them with us."

Drawing in a deep breath, she nodded.

"Foolish, but as you like," Salk snorted and turned. He paused only to glance over his shoulder at them. "My crew unloaded your delivery by your transporter. I believe you are more than capable of hauling it into your domicile. I hope that it is worth the credits spent to risk losing to a natural disaster," he spat.

"Many thanks, Salk. Always a pleasure to see you," Grish said to the male's retreating back.

"Boy, he *really* doesn't like you guys," Crystal observed.

"Bah, he is bitter. He did not pass the warrior trials. His sire assisted him in acquiring a position with the intergalactic transportation units. It was either that or devote several revolutions to another field," Grish volunteered.

"And for all his boasting about having a mate, she and his uthak share a closer relationship and spend through the majority of their domicile's income," Borth added. "But she is from an esteemed Teril family, so he considers himself fortunate."

A thought occurred to her, one that hadn't before. Although human females were considered a priceless commodity among species who lacked females, Terils weren't in that boat. It hurt to consider that she might be considered an inferior mate among them.

"Would you be considered better off if you had a Teril here rather than me?" she asked.

Borth glanced over at her with genuine surprise. "I would not care what they think. If I cared what anyone on Telif Prime thought, I would be there and not here on Antari Minor. I am happy here and with you. Yes, among most of our people, a Telif female is considered the ideal. I do not agree. My female before me is the ideal for me."

Comforted by that declaration, Crystal hugged his arm to her, accepting the sudden affection from them as they practically crushed her between them as they embraced her. Giggling, she pushed them back.

"Okay, so what's my surprise that was delivered?"

CHAPTER 23

Their female practically vibrated with glee as Grish connected their new intergalactic comm system to the long-range frequencies. It took up most of the spare room they had hauled the transportation containers into, but the smile on Crystal's face was worth it. They could always expand their domicile if they needed more rooms in the future. It wasn't like they had any offspring on the way, and as much as he would love to greet his own, he was not in a hurry. He was enjoying his time with their female.

And right now, their small human's excitement was infectious.

"I thought you said this would take six months to get here!"

Grish shrugged but was unable to hold back his smile. "When I saw how listless you were, I paid more credits to have it sent on a rushed shipment to arrive with the collector. I wanted to see this smile blooming on a face that was too often solemn."

She glanced up at him in surprise. "But that must have been weeks ago. You barely knew me. Why would you pay extra credits to get this here for me?"

"I did not know you very well yet, you are right, but in my

mind, you were my mate and I wanted to do anything to make you happy."

"It really does. Thank you!"

Standing on her toes, she dragged first his head down, and then his brother's, to give them each one of her soft, sweet-tasting kisses. The contact was brief, but Grish could feel the ache building as his cock began to swell. As she bounced on her toes and approached the comm system, Grish exchanged a meaningful look with his brother. Borth nodded in agreement, though he pressed his lips together anxiously.

"Have you given any further thought to accepting our mating bond?" he asked quietly, his eyes tracking her as she paced around the system, inspecting it thoroughly.

He could not unsee the way her back stiffened and the pause in her movements before she turned toward them. He wanted to close his eyes and not hear whatever she had to say. The pain that drew his heart's blood at least served the benefit of withdrawing the ache of budding arousal.

"Do not answer. Forget that I asked this foolish question. If you are not ready…" he rambled.

The press of Crystal's hand against his cheek silenced him as he met her eyes. Her gaze was full of longing, her front teeth sunk into her bottom lip, worrying at the delicate skin there until he dropped his head and placed his lips on hers to soothe reddening flesh. Drawing back slightly, he nuzzled his nose against hers, relishing the feel of her breath fanning against his face. His heart broke just a little when she pulled away.

"Grish, Borth…you have no idea how much I want to say yes. I just…can't. Not when this situation with the Calystii is hanging over me. It was different when I thought I could hide from them, but now that they know I'm here and now that I've fallen in love with you… I can't risk your happiness. I did some reading—you know how I am," she chuckled sadly, "I know that Terils only mate once in their lives. This would be it for you. I can't do that to you. That's why I refused when you came for me, not to punish you."

"But you speak as if mating would be a punishment for us," Borth growled. "Do you not understand that it would not matter, none of it, without you? Have we not made that clear?"

She swallowed, her eyes closing. "I just don't want to take your only chance."

Grish's heart constricted, but Borth was the one who moved first. He paced toward her, his red eyes burning as his large hand tipped her head up. "Look at me, *katna*."

Her eyes flickered open, her lips parting. "You have never called me that before."

"I have not. We have both been afraid, even afraid to speak this endearment in fear that you will not accept us as your mate in the end. But I am not anymore. Whether you give us this chance or not, this is our only choice. I am bound to you in heart if not by flesh. I do not care even if a thousand dangers seek us. I will face it all by your side as your mate if you will have us."

"You both feel that way?" she whispered.

"We do," Grish affirmed.

A tremulous smile curved her lips.

"And how do we go about doing this?"

Grish let out a relieved breath, elation driving out any lingering sadness as he realized exactly what she was saying.

"Typically, there is a small ceremony. We announce our intentions before family and friends before we take our female and bond her to us. That part is, of course, private between the uthak brothers and their female."

"That sounds nice," she murmured. "I know we're far from Telif Prime, but can we have a small ceremony anyway? It reminds me a little of wedding customs where the couple say their vows before family and friends. I wouldn't mind having Nargis and Talimia present to witness since they're our friends and helped us. Perhaps we can enjoy a celebratory dinner before we get to the mating part."

Grish nodded. "This is a good idea. It should be an occasion to be remembered. Perhaps our Arobi friends can attend, and any of our unit who are nearby. It would be a pleasure to share our joy with those we have once stood beside." He sighed as he looked forlornly at the trees. The leaves were falling more every day, and there was not even a flower remaining anywhere that in the summer grew in clusters around them. "A shame that winter is so near. I would love to crown you with flowers, as is our tradition."

Crystal wrapped her arms around his waist and hugged him to her before turning her embrace to Borth. "We can get creative, even just working with what we have. What's most important is having each other... for however long," she added quietly in afterthought.

"There is always a chance that time is cut short," Grish murmured down to her. "It is what we do with the time that counts, whether that be in battle or with those we love."

Pulling away, she grinned up at them, swiping her hands over her face. "All right. Enough of all this sentimental mush. Go find something constructive to do while I get to know my new toy."

Borth's lips upturned. "I believe we have just been replaced. Perhaps you did a little too well in pleasing our female," he teased.

"Small price to pay," Grish returned easily. "We will leave you alone with the comm, *katna.*"

She waved as they left the room and returned with a pair of virtual reality ocular lenses. With only a backward glance, she hopped into the leather seat, allowing herself to settle at an extreme angle as she placed the lenses over her eyes. A blue light sprung over them, data running as her fingers touched the comm controls.

Borth nudged him with his elbow. "Come, brother. Let us check for any further damages that may have occurred during the earthquake."

Nodding, Grish turned and followed his brother out of the room.

"At least the mess is smaller this time. It was a good idea to secure the storage units."

Borth chuckled, slanting him an amused look.

"That does not mean that there is nothing that requires our attention. We will take care of it while she enjoys herself a little in the systems. I have a feel that our upcoming mating will be keeping us all very busy," he said.

Borth was correct in that there was more to set to right than Grish had anticipated. Although the earthquake wasn't as strong as the first one, it was much stronger than the tiny tremors that had plagued them for weeks. It did not take them long, however, to straighten the disorder. They were just putting the last thing back in place as they navigated around Matida, who, disturbed by the earthquake, anxiously clung to their legs when Grish heard Crystal's footsteps as she entered the room.

He glanced up, but his smile of greeting died on his lips as he saw the pale, worried look on her face. She walked slowly toward him, nearly stumbling with shock. Even from where he stood, he could see the way her hands trembled.

"Borth!" he called to his brother in the next room. "There is something wrong with Crystal." He shelved a family tome before rushing with concern to her side. "*Katna*, what has happened?"

Eyes wide, she met his gaze, a shudder running over her before she leaned into him just as Borth burst into the room. The other male's eyes were frantic when they settled upon her, and he wasted no time in joining them, his hands brushing over her anxiously.

"*Katna*, speak to us and tell us what happened," Borth urged.

Crystal drew a deep breath and swallowed thickly. "You know that every few days I was going to visit Talimia…"

"Yes, of course. Something that we have approved and supported."

"When I'm there, I always check for any encrypted messages from the Lorgor resistance. There hasn't been any word, and I'd been starting to think that that no news is good news. I hoped that, just maybe, there was a small chance it would just go away."

"Crystal…"

She pressed against him, burying her face against him. A weak laugh escaped her, and she shook her head in what he could only presume was meant to be denial.

"I should have known better. I do know better than to hope something like that. Here I was, flitting around the systems, enjoying my gift and amusing myself. I decided at random to check again… This time, there was something."

"What message did they leave?" Borth growled with unease.

"They intercepted a communication. Apparently the Calystii looking for me do not know where I am…"

"But this is good news," Grish protested.

A bark of laughter escaped her.

"No, it isn't. The only reason they don't know my location is because they're receiving a comm from someone looking to collect a bounty on recovering me. The bounty hunter has arranged to meet them—with me in tow—at a space station in a matter of days. The Lorgors say to be on watch. The resistance is going to take advantage of the arranged meeting in order to trap and capture the Calystii Imperial Flagship, but they want us to go underground—to hide. They're still hoping to find Robby with my help once they narrow down his location to retrieve whatever he has. The Lorgors are certain he has something capable of crippling their enemy."

Borth swung around, roaring as he swung his fist into the

wall, punching a hole into the material. Grish frowned after his brother's show of rage in front of their female, but he couldn't deny that he wanted to do the same. Anything to vent the rage and frustration stirring within him. His hands tightened briefly on Crystal before he forced himself to loosen his grip with a murmur of apology.

Crystal stroked her hand against his arm. "It's okay. You didn't hurt me." She sighed and pinched the bridge of her nose. "I can't believe someone is collecting a bounty on me."

"It could be Danya. He saw you with us," Grish growled.

"Then he made a big mistake," Borth rumbled upon rejoining them. "I will go into town personally and hunt him down in his offices. He will not have an opportunity to regret targeting our mate."

Grish nodded grimly. "Take care of it early in the morning, brother, before the crowds thicken. I will remain here and guard Crystal. No one will get anywhere near our property. Especially not with Matida on the grounds. We will await your return."

Borth inclined his head, and between them, they folded their female in close, secure in the protection of their bodies. They would not relax their guard that night. This was the purpose that the uthak bond served. They would take shifts sleeping and guarding their mate to ensure that no harm would come to her.

No one would take their mate from them and live.

CHAPTER 24

Borth prowled through the streets in the faint light of the early morning. There were a few early risers moving around town, but they did not receive more than his fleeting notice as he approached the gleaming building of the local outpost of the Megaraisi Corporation. His tail stiffened as he neared, all his instincts on the attack.

He would not knock, and this would be no pleasant visit.

The moment he came within charging distance, Borth dropped his body low, throwing his whole mass into the metal door. Fueled by his rage, the simple metal of the office door not only crumpled beneath the force of his body but snapped free of the mechanisms that held it in place. It fell with a loud crash to the expensive stone floors, preceding the heavy thump of his footsteps as he entered.

A Calystii male hunkered low behind the reception desk, trembling with fear. Borth's gaze fixed on him, and he shook his head in warning. The male, apparently with an appreciation for being among the living, stepped away and fled from the building without a sound, leaving Borth alone in the lobby.

A rumble started in his throat, his eyes scanning the space

around him as he made his way deeper into the building. His gaze fell upon a small datascreen on the wall, and he pulled to a stop in front of it. Cocking his head, Borth ran his first finger down the menu, searching for the one familiar name among the many listed. Coming to it, he selected it, his hand flattening against the screen as his comm recorded the route in the large building to the male's office.

Borth turned away from the screen and headed along the corridors until he arrived at the correct door. With one well-placed kick, the polished wooden door coveted by the Calystii flew inward, hitting the floor with a hard slam, and Borth's eyes met the horrified gaze of his target.

Snarling, Borth stepped forward, his tail swinging behind him, his corded muscles standing out as his body tensed. Danya gasped and scrambled away, but despite the limberness of the species, he did not have enough distance to adequately escape Borth. One thick hand grabbed ahold of the Calystii, drawing him back sharply into his chair. A loud bark of surprise left the male's mouth, his eyes widening as Borth leaned in, his temper fit to murder the male if he so much as spoke the wrong way about Crystal.

"Wh…what do you want?" Danya gasped.

Borth did not answer him right away. Instead, he fixed his eyes on the male, well aware that the peculiar reddish pigment of his eyes tended to put many species at unease. Truthfully, many of this own species found it unnerving as well. It had caused him some heartache in his youth, but in instances such as this, it served him well.

"You like causing trouble. First for my Arobi friends and now for my uthak brother. I am not the sort of male to be patient with foolishness, who will let you escape freely despite the wrongs you have done."

"I did nothing—I swear!"

"Did you not threaten my mate?" he growled.

The Calystii paled an unhealthy pale hue, and he shook his head rapidly.

"No. I did not. I mean, yes, I tried to intimidate her. She looked familiar, and I thought that if I worked it to my advantage that I would ensure the cooperation of your family and the assimilation of your farm into our corporation. I swear, that is all I wanted."

"You are lying to me," Borth growled as he pressed forward, his weight coming down on the male's arm as he gripped his shoulder in his large hand.

"I am not. I promise you. That is all! I would not risk myself by doing something so stupid that it would endanger my life!"

"Then who has a bounty contract in agreement with the Imperial Calystii flagship heading toward this planet?" he snarled.

If it were possible, the male became even paler.

"They are coming here? No one in this office would make any arrangements with the Imperial family."

Borth leaned forward, his eyes narrowing suspiciously.

"And why should I believe this?"

"Because," the male gasped beneath the hold that had shifted up around his throat, "the corporation works outside of the mandates and permission of the Imperial family. It is Calystii-owned but not affiliated with our homeworld. In order to increase our legitimacy, we have illegal paperwork forged saying that we have the emperor's blessing to establish territories and collect payment on behalf of the Empire for the goods we are distributing… and we sell them at full cost, for profit to our own people," he added weakly. "That alone violates several laws dealing with goods dispersal that are disadvantageous to an enterprising merchant. My employers depend on *not* being within range of the Imperial powers."

"Then *who* would have a bounty on my mate with an arrangement to fulfill it within the next few days?"

A calculating look crossed the male's face until Borth squeezed hard enough to be a sufficient reminder that the Calystii not get any ideas.

Danya growled helplessly within his grasp. "Nikana," he snarled. "I only recently learned that the retired Imperial bounty hunter had come to this shithole planet. The payment that the Imperial family was offering is exactly what would draw the Morith into action."

Borth looked down at the male in disbelief. *Nikana?* The female was trusted by nearly everyone who traversed at one point or another through Intakfell. She had even been there, newly established, when he and his brother arrived.

"Impossible!"

The male in his grasp chuckled. "Why? Because of her kindness? Nikana can slip a blade into her victim's back while certain that he is smiling and unsuspecting the entire time."

Borth dropped the male, his body swinging around so fast that the Calystii didn't have time to evade his tail as it slapped him to the ground. That was unintentional, but Borth did not regret it. He did not even give it a second thought as he opened his comm.

"Grish, we have a problem… Grish? Answer your comm!"

The Calystii pushed himself up to his knees and gave him a sympathetic look. "If she has already moved to strike, then you are too late."

The male's cocky smile suddenly disappeared as the earth jerked, and he shouted fearfully as a vicious earthquake rattled the building, breaking windows and demolishing everything that was flung with great strength to the ground.

"Get off this planet if you have any sense of self-preservation," Borth snarled as he rose once more to his feet. "This is the only warning I will give you."

He did not waste any more words on the male as he rushed out of the building to his flyer. Panic was setting in as he tried repeatedly to raise Grish and Crystal on their comms. Why were they not answering? A shudder ran over his skin as his eyes tracked to the volcano that appeared to have increased in size, a lick of dread sliding down his spine.

"Answer!" he snarled as he slid into the flyer.

CHAPTER 25

Crystal frowned from where she stood in the common room. It hadn't been that long ago when she had stood there, singing with boredom. Now she was anything but bored, her muscles tight and achy with tension. She was genuinely afraid, but also felt a kernel of real anger setting in.

She had worked hard and built a life on Antari Minor with Borth and Grish. She resented like hell that the Calystii were now going to ruin everything.

From the corner of her eye, she saw Grish re-enter the room, his tail stiff behind him. It reminded her of sexytimes with the guys, but she knew that the context was very different this time. Grish's entire body was on alert to kill anything or anyone who attempted to enter their home.

His beautiful amber eyes met her gaze. He attempted to give her a comforting smile, but it was tight with worry. She gave him props for at least trying, however. Walking over to her side, he grazed his knuckles against her cheek soothingly.

"Nargis commed in a panic before static interference dropped the communication. I could not make out much of what he said, but he spoke of seeing something suspicious moving through his property. I am going to head out that way for only a minute. Borth will already be in town by now dealing with Danya, so there should not be anything for you to worry about. Still, stay here and be safe until I return. Just be cautious. Remember that Matida is out there, so it is unlikely that anyone will be able to get anywhere near the property."

She nodded mutely, her heart pattering at a rapid tempo in her chest. There was no reason to be so scared. He was right. This was all going to be over soon; he was just going to follow the lead on an intruder. All she needed to do was remain there.

She could do that.

"I'll be fine," she croaked.

"I will be back very soon. Stay inside," he reiterated, and pressed a blaster into her hand. "If anything happens, protect yourself by any means necessary."

She produced a weak smile and gave him a thumbs up. "You got it, dude."

Confused amber eyes blinked at her, and she sighed.

"Don't worry about it… It's just a thing. Everything and everyone is, dude. I'm just rambling out of panic here, so don't mind me."

His expression softened, and he nuzzled her.

"Hurry back, Grish," she whispered. "I'm not going to lie. All this shit is creeping me out. Especially the comms suddenly not working."

"Static interference is uncommon, but has been known to happen," he said. "Do not worry, *katna*, I prefer your company to all others and will rush back at my greatest speed."

She chuckled, her head tilting up to meet his embrace as he lowered his head to drop a kiss on her lips. She felt marginally better about the situation minutes later when he exited the house, his enormous bulk dwarfing everything around him as he headed to the stable to get his gorthal. When he emerged mounted on the large animal, it skittered nervously, its head tossing before it ran at full gallop in the direction of Nargis's farm.

She sighed. A stupid Calystii wasn't going to be able to get past that male.

Wrapping her arms around herself, Crystal licked her lips and settled in, resting her bottom against the arm of the couch as she stared out at the familiar scenery.

He would only be gone for a little while. He would be coming back through the adjoining orchards before she knew it.

She stood there, leaning against the couch, until restlessness drove her to pace back and forth through the common room. The absolute silence of the house settled around her with such familiarity that when a knock sounded at the door she nearly jumped out of her skin.

Her hand darted to the blaster, the small hairs at the back of her neck practically standing on end. She listened, waiting for the ferocious sound of Matida attacking, but was met with silence. *Odd.*

A laugh bubbled out of her. Her paranoia was showing. How many killers or bounty hunters were going to politely knock as if it were a Sunday social visit?

The knock started again.

"Crystal? Are you home?" a familiar voice called sweetly.

"Nikana, what are you doing here?" Crystal called through the door as she arrived in front of it. Through the doorway cam, she saw the female grimace apologetically at the door.

"I apologize for arriving so suddenly. I tried to call on my way over, but it seems that comms are acting up again. I just had to come, however. I feel it is a matter of some import. I heard some talk at the teahouse that I thought you should know about. Especially after your meeting with the Lorgors... May I come in?"

An amused huff burst from her. "Of course, Nikana. I'm sorry.

Give me a minute and I'll disarm the security systems. Is Matida there with you?"

"Hmm? No, I haven't seen her yet. Perhaps she is sniffing out something that attracted her attention. Smart of your mates to have her wandering nearby, however. Things are not safe right now."

Nikana could say that again. It bothered her a little that Matida didn't alert her to the Morith's approach, but Crystal shrugged, unconcerned. The animal was rarely flighty, but Nikana wasn't a threat, and it wasn't unheard of for the animal to follow her nose and do as she liked on a whim.

Security disabled, Crystal put a hand on the locking panel beside the door and waited as it read her biometric signature. The door slipped open with a click, and a familiar golden female stepped inside.

"Oh, thank the gods," the female breathed, scrubbing her arms to knock loose the leaves that had fallen over the long, poncho-like cover draped over her robes. "I appreciate you opening your home to me."

"It's no problem," Crystal assured her. "You've always been so kind, even to an awkward offworlder like me—not enough time developing people skills, I'm afraid," she chuckled, "I do appreciate that you were willing to come all this way to warn me."

"Of course. Think nothing of it," the female said lightly, her eyes darting around. Crystal paused at the furtive look, but it disappeared, and the female smiled at her. "Speaking of your males, where are they? I thought I saw Grish in the distance heading off your property, but where is your handsome male, Borth?"

"He is in town following a lead," she answered as she gestured for the female to follow her into the kitchen. "We discovered that someone is collecting a bounty on me."

"Oh yes, I heard the same. I had to come the very moment I heard," Nikana said behind her as Crystal grabbed the pot to start brewing intimbar. The female had come all that way out of kindness. It was the least she could do.

Setting the pot on the heated plate, she rubbed her eyes wearily.

"Are you well?" the female asked softly.

"Yes, of course. Just tired. I didn't sleep well last night, and this whole thing has me anxious. I'll be grateful when it's over."

"I can imagine." Nikana's footsteps grew closer. "I do hope that Borth discovers the identity of the bounty hunter. It is very distressing, I am sure you know."

Crystal nodded and switched off the heated pot, the light trill from the heated water fading away as she set it aside.

"It's a little scary, but I think Borth knows who it is. Even so, they aren't taking any chances. Grish was pretty insistent that I stay locked down in here until he returned. He won't be too happy that I let you in, but I think he will be pretty understanding, knowing it's you."

"Perhaps not," Nikana said right behind her, something stirring within her voice that made all the fine hairs on Crystal raise with alarm. From her peripheral vision, she watched as a blaster rose to point in her direction. "In this case, you should have listened to your mate."

Adrenaline surged through her on a current of fear as Crystal pivoted around, swinging the pot hard enough that it collided with the Morith's face. The blaster flew off, clattering to the floor somewhere out of sight.

Crystal didn't wait around to hunt for it. With a hard shove, she pushed by Nikana, knocking the female to the floor with her curvier frame as she bolted for the front door. Her feet had no sooner hit the lavender grass when blaster fire erupted behind her.

"*Fuck!* Crazy bitch!" she shouted as she hauled ass to the stable.

Her sweet boy turned his head toward her at her sudden arrival. Clambering over to his side, she thanked Grish for patiently teaching her to ride before the final harvest, and pulled herself up onto his back.

Giving his head free rein, she shouted a command, her heels digging into his sides as he sprung forward, bursting from the stable. His quick step neatly evaded the blaster fire from the enraged, screaming Morith, as he carried her away from the property in the opposite direction from Nargis's farm.

She needed to get some distance between herself and the Morith *without* risking her mates. Her lips pressed into a thin line as she hoped to lose her pursuer through all the trees on the northeastern neighbor's farm, whose property ran right up to the base of the volcano. Nikana wouldn't be able to follow her by flyer through that dense growth.

She wanted to shout in triumph, and was just relaxing against Morosh as he ran spryly through the woods when the earth bucked beneath them, sending Crystal flying hard into a tree. As her head made contact, slamming into the thick trunk, a light flashed behind her eyelids. She was aware of the rustle of violently swaying trees only a moment before she dropped unconscious to the ground.

CHAPTER 26

Grish drew back sharply on the reins of his gorthal, Etuaan, forcing him to stop in front of the house. The animal fought him, his head tossing, the arcing horn spearing back as he attempted to break Grish's control. The earthquake had brought both him and the stallion down, but thankfully he had been quick enough to grab the reins before his mount could break and run. The animals had been anxiously milling around the stable, their breaths snorting out in billows when he fetched his mount just hours earlier.

He should have paid attention to the signs. There was no call for evacuation over the comms, but with the static interference, even if there were a last-minute emergency order to flee to safety, he wouldn't have received it. Likely the majority of farms outside of town would not have, either. His last comm had been the badly scrambled missive from Nargis. Or so he had thought, until the male had greeted his presence with surprise.

He had been lured away from the property at the worst possible time.

He had been deceived, and worse yet, they had been wrong!

There was no way that Danya would have been able to get

past Borth to their land. The bounty hunter working for the Calystii was someone else. He knew that without a doubt when he spun away from Nargis's domicile with a roar of rage.

Grish's anger was so great that he had barely been aware of his friend following him as he stalked away, until the male had grabbed his arm and insisted they stop at the stable for weapons. Grish hadn't been expecting much, shocked when the male opened a hidden wall at the back of the stable containing a large collection of blasters and plasma weapons. Nargis saddled a massive, shaggy four-horned oowali and holstered blasters with an ease that had been surprising for a Wanit after tossing Grish a blaster and a large plasma rifle.

They had ridden out, pushing their mounts as fast as possible until the earthquake had thrown them. Then a new fear had replaced his rage, and he sent his friend back to evacuate his mate. The volcano wasn't going to go back to sleep.

He had known that when he had sat up, reins firmly in hand, and had seen the evidence of the dead fish floating in the lake they were passing. Over the last few days, he had noted the presence of dead insects and birds randomly appearing on his property but hadn't thought much of it. Animals died all the time, especially in the cooling days and nights of the autumn. He should have remembered that deadly gasses were often released prior to eruptions.

Now a beat sounded within him that cried out *"too late, too late."*

"Crystal! Katna!" he shouted, steering his mount toward the door.

He would ride right in and grab her if he needed to. He opened his mouth again, prepared to verbally override the lock codes so he wouldn't have to dismount, but his heart seized with terror as the door slid open at his approach. It was unlocked.

He had locked it—he was certain!

"*Crystal!*" he bellowed with overwhelming rage and grief.

There was no answer, only silence, as he directed his gorthal inside. The wide structure of their domicile allowed easy passage. Nothing appeared disturbed except the kitchen, where an over-turned pot spilled water all over the floor. Drawing a deep breath, a hiss escaped him as a familiar scent lingering in the room slid over his olfactory receptors. A vicious snarl escaped him as hate rose sharp and hungry in his mind with the identity of the betrayer becoming at once clear to him.

Nikana.

Revolutions of friendship between them with every visit to her teahouse, and she had betrayed it to collect a bounty on their mate.

Throwing his head back, he bellowed, his roar echoing through the house as he drove his mount forward. Etuuan sprung forward with a deep, resonating bark. The animal's heavy hooves clattered over the floor as they raced back through the domicile and burst back out the door. A heavy shadow immediately drew up ahead of him, and Grish's arm snapped up, leveling the plasma rifle at the intruder.

"Grish, put the rifle down," Borth snarled, stepping forward from the shadows, his arms laden with a heavily sedated tantogal. "She is not here or anywhere on the property. I have been searching for her and any sign of Nikana since I arrived a short time ago."

"And Matida?" Grish rasped.

"Fine. Just sleeping. I found her just behind the stable."

Grish nodded. "Good. Get her and the animals in the cargo of the flyer. We have to leave immediately."

"Into the flyer? Grish, there is barely room in the cargo for animals this big," Borth said. "It wouldn't be safe to transport them this way once we catch up to Crystal. I am certain she escaped Nikana. Her mount is gone."

Relief surged through Grish, but he knew it wouldn't last long if they did not hurry to find their mate. His hand shot forward as he grabbed ahold of his brother's shirt.

"Borth, we do not have a choice. The volcano…"

The male's eyes widened in horror as understanding dawned and he yanked free. Working quickly, they secured the two gorthals in their flyer's cargo bay and hauled Matida into the passenger area. The tantogal took up half of the available space, but leaving the animals behind was not an option. They had promised their mate. The only difference was that they no longer had the option to use the transporter.

"Do you know in what direction she rode out?" Grish asked as he slid into the pilot's seat.

"Yes, due northeast into the timber farm," Borth replied in a broken voice as he dropped down beside him.

"She went straight toward the volcano?" Grish snarled in alarm.

His brother dragged a hand down his face wearily. "It was the route that we advised her to take if she needed to escape from the emergency exit, was it not?"

Snarling an oath, Grish initialized flight, the flyer steadily rising in the sky. They were only just aloft, heading toward the lumber fields, when an explosive crack shook the world around them, the burst sending the flyer spinning out of control.

Muscles straining, Grish fought against the controls, ignoring the panicked barks and bellows of the gorthals in the back. At his side, Borth grabbed the co-pilot emergency controls and in tandem, they drew upon their emergency training to stabilize the flyer.

Putting the flyer back on the route, he increased the engine speed, eyes on the column of smoke and fire bursting from the mouth of the volcano. The ash was already starting to fall, but he wasn't worried about that. The engine possessed advanced fine-particle filters. The ash would not bring down the flyer. What he was more concerned about were the ballistics that would potentially be flying through the air at them.

The bright flare of magma spilling from the volcano became more visible the closer they flew. Streaking over the forest below, however, was filling him with concern as he realized that the farm grounds were right in the path of the lava flow. As the acres of trees passed farther and farther behind them, he felt a low anxiety burning in his belly.

How were they going to find their mate in time?

"There, a flash of gold… Do you see it? That is Morosh. I am certain of it," Borth exclaimed suddenly, his hands flying over the controls, taking full command of the landing sequencing before Grish could react.

Shaking himself from the sorrow that had descended over him, Grish squinted against the gloom, his heart picking up as he saw the familiar flash of wooly golden fur. His breath seizing in his chest, he powered up the blasters and aimed them to a small stretch of land within close proximity to the sighting.

Although the scans on the ship weren't working as well as he would like, a sharp breath of relief shot out of him when he was able to pick up the faint signatures of the gorthal, their mate and another directly to the side of the flyer.

Snarling low in his throat, Grish scanned the tree-line for an open landing area. He could level the trees, but it would attract too much attention. His eyes immediately settled on a small clearing a short distance away. It really was not quite big enough for their ship, but he could make it work. He had done so in smaller spaces when he did emergency evacs during his service in the fleet. They would drop down in stealth mode so as not to alert the bounty hunter, but would only have a limited amount of time to locate Crystal.

CHAPTER 27

Crystal blinked, a wave of nausea flowing through her. She wanted to close her eyes and wait for it to pass. Fuck, her head hurt. Eyes tearing up, she felt the brush of something warm against her face. Despite the pain in her head, she turned it to look over at the gold muzzle mouthing her anxiously.

What was she doing outside on the ground? Hand shaking, she lifted it and set it against the fuzzy fur as everything came flooding back to her.

Nikana.

She couldn't just lie around; she had to get out of there. Groaning, she sat up and coughed, powder puffing from her lips. Glancing down at herself, her mind blanked out in horror as she stared down at the white ash coating her. She glanced over at Morosh, and while it wasn't as obvious on the gorthal due to his thick wool, she could see signs of his coat dulling from it. Ash… It was falling from the sky!

With a muffled cry, she stumbled to her feet, her hand gripping the reins. Morosh backed up slowly, his weight helping to pull her up. She wanted to cry in gratitude and made a mental note to thank the breeder who offered him to her. Although the animal was obviously terrified and ready to bolt, he hadn't left her side.

"Good boy," she whispered, her hand patting his thick cheek.

Looking around slowly, a shudder overcame her, her eyes trailing to the mountain—or rather the volcano spewing smoke and heat into the sky. Tiny red embers lit the pyroclastic cloud rolling out from the summit. Her nostrils flared, taking the scent of sulfur and the horrifying smell of burning trees.

The lumber farm was on fire!

"Fuck!" she hissed, scurrying around the side of the gorthal, hands gripping the saddle.

"Do not move," Nikana's voice ordered sharply.

Muscles tensing to the point of shaking with terror, Crystal froze, only turning her head enough to look over at the Morith female stumbling from a hoverbike settled between two trees. The blaster pointed at her didn't so much as waver as the female stalked toward her. Crystal licked her lips. This was insane!

"Nikana, please," she croaked. "I don't know what I did but please don't do this. We need to get out of here. The trees are on fire and…"

"Be silent, human," Nikana growled, any trace of anything maternal or friendly that Crystal had once seen absent and replaced with a hard, merciless stare. "I admit that I was not eager to come out of retirement. I am content with my teahouse, but as I said, business has been a little slow lately. The Calystii offered a considerable bounty on you—one I could not pass up." A tiny flash of remorse flashed over the female's face. "It is nothing personal. I really do like you, and it is true that I want to see more females arrive here. But this… this is business. You understand, I am sure. We are both females who have done what we needed to do to survive."

"But I've never hurt anyone. Please, we can pay you. We just pulled in a good harvest—I'll buy out my contract. I just want to be with my mates."

Nikana snorted. "Even with your harvest, it would not be more than a pittance compared to the hundreds of thousands of credits I am getting in exchange for you. I admire your attempt to negotiate, but no. Come quietly, human. If I need to shoot, I will. Make no mistake about that."

"What's wrong with you? We're standing in the path of an active volcano!" Crystal snapped. "Do you have a death wish? We should be running for our fucking lives and you have a blaster trained on me."

The female shrugged. "A bounty comes with risks, but it always pays off. Now are you coming quietly, or do I lame you, possibly paralyze you, and drag you away?"

Crystal took a step back and heard a blaster firing up as the Morith's eyes narrowed mercilessly on her. The sound was covered by a crackling roar, and Crystal's eyes swung up, fixing on the ball of flaming molten rock shooting through the air.

"Oh my fucking gods," she whispered as Nikana's gaze also shot up.

Hugging the side of her gorthal and ducking low, Crystal's entire body shook as the fireball hit a nearby cluster of trees. Flames burst, and sparks fell dangerously around them. Nikana dodged, her eyes widening at the immediate danger threatening them.

A burst of plasma fire came from out of nowhere, catching the Morith off guard as it struck the tree just behind her, grazing her in the process. The female hissed in pain, her hand clutching at the stripe of blackened fabric on her side as she bared her teeth at someone off to Crystal's left.

"Drop your weapon and back away, Nikana," Borth growled.

The Morith hissed, but as he raised another blaster and the laser light of a plasma rifle fastened on her from another angle, she tossed her blaster aside and backed away, her eyes glinting with promised vengeance.

Crystal jumped as she was suddenly picked up off her feet, but the gentle rumble that came from behind her swept over her in a welcome familiarity. Grish's solid arms tightened around her as he shuffled her out of harm's way. She tightened her own grip on Morosh's reins so that he moved away with them, the animal snorting and tossing his head uneasily, his dark eyes rolling with fear.

"Easy," Grish rumbled.

She wasn't sure if that was more for her benefit or for the animal's, but she attempted to regulate her breathing despite her terror. She could see a red light infusing the forest as an intense heat licked over her skin. Fire was racing up trees, but she was fairly certain that she could see the destructive glide of magma as it slowly consumed everything in its path. She panted, her lungs burning from the gasses released into the air. She wanted to flee as her fear climbed, but Grish's arms kept her firmly in place as he backed them through the trees until they exited into a small clearing.

Just ahead of them, Borth paced backward, his weapon still leveled on Nikana, providing cover as Grish lifted her completely off her feet. Then she was smothered between the press of wooly gorthals, Morosh making a plaintive sound as he was tugged in between his larger stablemates.

The moment they were in, Grish's hand slammed against a panel, closing the cargo bay before racing into the passenger area with Crystal still against his chest. Stepping over a sleeping Matida, he set her quickly in a chair and strapped her in before leaping into the pilot's seat. She wheezed, attempting to draw in big lungfuls of the clean, filtered air within the flyer, her eyes fastened on the front viewing screen.

Borth was nearly at the nose of the flyer, his blaster firmly on

Nikana, when the female erupted into action. With a piercing shriek that was common to her species, she lunged at him, her hands gripping his weapon as she attempted to rip it from his hand. They fought for the weapon for only a second. Although Borth had been caught by surprise, his greater bulk allowed him to fling the female aside, losing his grip on the blaster in the process. Crystal watched the female fall to the ground, the blaster hitting the ground near her as Borth spun around and hurried to the flyer.

The door slid open as he gripped the opening with one hand and swung himself inside, bypassing the ramp. Grish's hand slammed on the control, initiating take off, and the door sealed shut with the loud rumble of the engines firing up. The red glow was rapidly approaching, pyroclastic bombs falling, striking trees, some of them already on fire and adding to the chaos. Volcanic lightning flickered through the darkening sky, but Crystal could still clearly see Nikana as the female scrambled for the weapon and leaped to her feet. Raising the blaster, she fired several times at the flyer, and it rocked as one shot made contact. Grish's lips thinned, but he increased velocity as the flyer shot away from the female.

Crystal couldn't look away. She watched as the female lowered her arm, her head snapping left and right as the fire and magma advanced toward her. With a choked cry, Crystal shut her eyes against the sight of the female being consumed and was grateful that she couldn't hear the screams as the flyer sped away.

She didn't open her eyes again until she felt the nudge of Matida's scaled nose on her hand. Her cheeks felt wet as she looked down at the tantogal staring up at her with bright golden eyes, and she lifted a hand to wipe them away. Clearing her throat, she looked back at the viewing screen as the flyer drifted over the land, and she was able to see their own farmhouse.

Already flames were licking at the outer edge of their property, and she blinked back tears.

Borth glanced back and, noting her expression, he unfastened himself from the copilot chair and pushed back between the seats until he was able to crouch in front of her.

"Are you well, *katna*?" he murmured, his large hand cupping the side of her face. Worry darkened his amber red eyes, and she dredged up a smile.

"Yes," she rasped. "My throat hurts a little... from the gasses, I think, but I'm okay. The farm though..." Her voice dropped away as tears threatened again, and she swallowed thickly.

Leaning forward, Borth nuzzled her, his breath hot on her ear.

"Everything can be replaced. The harvest has been pulled in, and any damage that the volcano does will make the land even more fertile for planting. All that matters to us is that you are safe."

She nodded. "What if the house burns?"

"Then we will build a better one," Grish replied from the pilot's seat.

He glanced back at her over his shoulder and gave her a smile full of love that had her heart stuttering. The same love she could see reflected back to her through Borth's eyes.

They were right. Despite everything, they had each other.

"And you do not need to worry about the Calystii," Borth said, his smile widening. "Nikana was so eager to collect the bounty that the Imperial family do not know you are here, and the Megaraisi Corporation will no longer be a problem anywhere near this territory. You will be safe, *katna*."

She let out a shaky breath, relief making her limbs go weak.

"Safe," she whispered in awe. Blinking away her tears as their house faded away into the distance, she looked over at her males. "Where are we going to go now?"

"We have friends," Grish replied. "I have sent Nargis and

Talimia in their direction already when I realized what was happening. They will meet us there. The Arobis and their mate will have space. We will contact them once we are within range so they will know to expect our arrival."

"How long do you think it'll be before we will know when we can go home?" she asked softly.

Borth raised his brows and shrugged. "Home is wherever our mate is. If you will still have us."

A soft laugh escaped her, and she nodded as she looked into the rough, loving faces of her males. There was little softness about the Terils physically, but their eyes and the gentle smiles on their lips conveyed it.

She didn't want to spend another moment without knowing that they were hers in every way.

"I wouldn't have it any other way."

Crystal had objected to needing a ceremony to accept her mates. After everything they had been through, and the fact that they were intruding on the Arobi and their wonderful mate, Hayley, she didn't want anyone to go through the trouble.

It was enough that they were together.

To her surprise, when they announced their intention to mate, Hayley and one of her formidable-looking mates, a male with scars lacing him, took to the kitchen with the insistence that it was an occasion worthy of a celebratory feast.

And that was how she found herself in the midst of a small mating ceremony among her new friends, and their Wanit friends, who had also made it to the safety of the Arobi's property.

Talimia was all smiles as she and Hayley helped Crystal get ready, the Wanit female producing a beautiful hair wreath, not of flowers but golden leaves and the sort of nuts and berries common in the late autumn on Antari Minor. With their help, and a borrowed robe from Hayley, Crystal felt as beautiful as a real bride when she joined her mates outside beneath an arch wrapped in ribbons and clusters of the remaining splendors of autumn.

The simple declaration of their intention to mate before their family and friends was greeted with cheers, the pouring of copious amounts of a sort of unfamiliar mulled wine that enchanted her taste buds, and a feast in their honor that she wouldn't have imagined just days earlier when they were escaping with their lives.

Her heart felt full of joy when at last they retired. Every moment during the day, every pleasure and happiness had culminated in this moment now that she was kneeling nude on the bed between her mates.

Their eyes caressed her, heating her flesh without them even needing to touch her. She needed their touch. She needed to feel totally claimed by them, now and forever. She wiggled, knowing that her sex was releasing pheromones by the way her mates' nostrils flared and their pupils dilated in awareness.

They did not reach for her, though.

Instead, they reached to a spot just under their jaw at their throat and she watched in fascination as each male placed a dark nail beneath a thin ridge. Then she saw it wasn't a ridge in their scales, but a thin barb flattened between them. They winced as they tugged the barb free, small droplets of blood appearing on the scales. She nearly shot off the bed, thinking they were injured, but Borth held her still and Grish gave her a sweet smile.

Holding the barb out for her inspection, his deep voice rolled over her.

"A Teril is only born with one chance, a single barb with which he can pierce his mate and bind us with the released bonding chemicals. Will you accept our barbs?"

Relaxing, she eyed the barb, but nodded. She wanted it. The idea of being pierced was surprising, but she wanted this with every part of her being.

A smile spread across Grish's face, and he tilted her head back gently.

"Just remain there, like that," he murmured.

The prick of first one barb and then the other made her eyes water, but no more than the prick of a needle. Immediately following, however, was a hot rush of desire as whatever chemicals were in the barbs were unleashed into her body. Bonding chemicals swept through her, preparing her body, as heat gathered in her sex. It was almost like the chemical release she'd experienced the first time Borth and Grish claimed her together during the height of her fertile period.

She had been a little disappointed when, during the harvest, her monthly had come, but in retrospect there was too much to be done to be thinking about babies right now.

Although their farmhouse had been spared from the lava flow and fires, much of their property—acres upon acres of land—hadn't fared so well when the reports came in the day before. She had arranged for birth control the same day, and it was partially why she felt she could safely enjoy the thrill of hormones punching through her system in reaction to the dual stings.

Her flesh heating unbearably, she twisted between them, her hips jerking in desperate need for relief. Her mates didn't lose any time embracing her between them, mouths dropping upon her, eagerly tasting her body as she writhed, little whines escaping her that would have been mortifying if they weren't all lost in the lust soaring through them. Her pheromones were feeding their need until they were nearly as mindless as she was.

Pinned between them, she felt a sharp stab of welcome pleasure-pain as first Grish and then Borth plunged within her sex. Her pussy was swollen and extra flexible as before, taking both males with only the slight burn of discomfort that gave way to intense pleasure as their bodies rocked against each other. The fire climbed through her, the bodies of her mates pressing against her feeling like infernos as they all succumbed to the intense consuming fires of their mating.

When at last their flames erupted, joining them together

forever, they collapsed on the bed, bodies damp with perspiration and breaths ragged. She smiled when her males cuddled close to her. As they lay there, Borth's voice rumbled against her ear where it was resting against his chest.

"I was thinking… It will take time before our farm is ready for us to return and seed it. It may be a good idea to hire a manager to see to it and watch over the crops for a short time… perhaps half a year, or a full year if necessary."

Crystal glanced up as she felt Grish's responding smile where his mouth was still pressed against her shoulder.

"For what?"

Her male gave her a crafty look, grinning. "I was just thinking that I might like to get my leg fixed and see about taking care of a small detail."

Her brows knit in confusion even as a flicker of excitement lit through her. It sounded almost like he had some sort of adventure in mind before they returned to settle down on their little farm.

"What do you have in mind?" she asked.

"That the Lorgor are right that you may be able to help find this Robby male," he answered, his eyes gleaming down at her.

Her lips split into a wide smile as she leaned more comfortably in their embrace.

"A little payback sounds good," she said on a laugh, surrounded in the comfort and supporting love of her males. It was about time to take ahold of her future.

EPILOGUE 2

*R*obby Dennison pulled his hood up higher over his head. The space station was crowded, but it was better than being planet-bound. From the space station, he could go anywhere. Plus there were a lot of opportunities for someone of his particular… talents.

Things had relaxed recently when he heard that the Lorgor resistance captured an Imperial flagship. It hadn't taken him much digging to discover it was the same ship he'd stolen the codex from. He grinned to himself and patted his pocket.

Amazing what one small chip could have on it—a tiny chip that the prince wasn't even supposed to have in his custody. It had been smuggled onto the ship by a Lorgor rebel. It contained all the flight routes, as well as the known and unknown outposts of the Calystii Empire. The rebel had risked his life to transport it from Caysa.

Some males were fools to put their necks on the line.

When Robby had been hired by the resistance, the male's cover had already been blown, and he had no doubt been caught and executed after the ugly alien handed it over into his care.

Robby had been contracted to meet the resistance, but he had second thoughts.

Why hand it over when he could sell it for infinitely more to a private buyer?

It was bound to be worth a lot of credits, and now that the prince was seized and had been executed by the resistance for crimes against the Lorgor people, the secret of what he had stolen went with him.

The only thing that had helped Robby evade capture for so long was the fact that the spoiled prince was terrified of telling his family of what had been smuggled and stolen. Gossip among Lorgors on leave from the flagship said that the prince had been determined to retrieve it himself. He had done Robby a favor. Of course, it helped that Robby had thrown Crystal into their path by leaving a false trail back to their apartment.

It was a shame about that, but he had a feeling she was getting ready to dump his ass anyway, and he needed to keep the Calystii distracted.

As far as he could tell, it had done a good enough job. The prince had even put out the bounties with his own money without the knowledge and consent of the Imperial family as he divided his attention in multiple directions trying to track them. Although Robby heard rumors that Crystal had made it off the planet, he wasn't sure how long she made it, or if she was even still alive.

It wasn't his problem, of course, and now the prince was dead for his trouble, and Robby was in the clear.

Grinning to himself, he almost had a bounce in his step, his eyes scanning for the place that he had arranged to meet his buyer. He had been clever, targeting his buyer, and now he was finally getting the huge payday and everything that was owed to him for all the hassle he had gone through over the years.

His eyes lit up as he arrived at his destination.

Ninawellas flashed with prisms of surging lights, teasing his senses along with the intoxicating scent of liquor and spice. Spice was fine, but not quite what he enjoyed indulging in. But where there was spice, one could find a wealth of more entertaining substances.

But first, his client.

His eyes trailed through the place until they landed on a male matching the description he was looking for. The Teril was huge, clearly not of a distinguished house or part of the Fleet, with that artificial leg. It was a quality prosthetic, however, which told him that the male had money. Everything about him stated that he was the well-paid bounty hunter that Robby was told that he would be meeting to make the exchange.

His palms dampened slightly with nerves. It was a tingle of intimidation as he drew closer to the enormous male, and excitement strumming through his system, perhaps sharpened by the remaining traces of uvoli—more potent than any crack found on Earth—rushing through his veins.

The male's creepy reddish eyes narrowed on him, but the male didn't speak. Instead, he jerked his head, indicating that he should follow him to the back room. Exactly as he expected. This wasn't his first time running illegal goods for aliens since his escape into space, and the rote familiarity sang in his blood with a building thrill.

Ducking into the darkened room, he paused with uncertainty when a light flared, illuminating part of the room. He faltered at the second enormous form of a hooded Teril waiting in the room, distinct by his size and the huge tail jutting stiffly from beneath the robes.

Robby cleared his throat as he began to creep back toward the door.

"I think there's been a mistake," he whispered.

The Teril who had met him grinned humorlessly, eyes glinting with a hidden fire in their depths.

"No mistake except your own," he rumbled with menace.

Robby's pulse pounded, his heart pinching as if it were about to burst from his chest.

"What's wrong, Robby?" a familiar feminine voice murmured.

A smaller hooded figure pushed out from behind the second male, and a pair of human hands lifted to tug back the hood. Relief punched him in the gut, and his breath whooshed out of him in a shaky laugh.

Crystal, however, wasn't smiling except for the tiniest tilt at one corner of her mouth.

"Crystal—*fuck*—you scared the shit out of me! You don't know how happy I am to see you alive."

A dark eyebrow raised.

"Why is that? Oh, I know. It's because you led them to my door and left me to take the fall for your stupidity. Right?"

"It wasn't personal, sweetheart. Just business."

"Just business. Funny that you're not the first person to say that to me lately. But I do understand, and that's why I know you will appreciate the irony of your situation. It seems you've been a very, very bad boy running off with something that the Lorgor paid you a lot of credits to retrieve and transport for them."

He paled, a cold sweat breaking out over his body.

"What are you saying…?"

"Nothing at all. Just that I believe you have some unfinished business," she said, her lips finally parting in a smile as she turned and waved forward someone he hadn't seen in the darker shadows at the rear of the room.

Robby felt faint as an enormous Lorgor strode toward him, violet eyes blazing down at him coldly and without sympathy. Robby turned a beseeching look to Crystal.

"Crystal, please. Don't do this. You don't know what the rebellion might do to me. You can't just let them have me!"

Her lips pursed and the two Teril males flanking her growled at him in obvious threat.

"Sorry, Robby. But as you say... it *is* just business."

<u>The Mate Index</u>
First Contact
The VaDorok
Hearts of Indesh (Valentine Novella)
The Edoka's Destiny
The Vori's Mate
Eliza's Miracle (Novella)
A Kiss on Kaidava
The Vori's Secret
A Mate for Oigr (Halloween Novella)
Heart of the Agraak
A Gift for Medif
The Arobi's Queen
Teril's Fire

<u>Monsterly Yours</u>
The Orc Wife
The Troll Bride
The Accidental Werewolf's Mate
<u>Love Blooms for the Pixie Queen (coming Sept 2020)</u>

The Unicorn's Mare (coming Dec 2020)

Sci-Fi Fairytales
Red: A Dystopian World Alien Romance
The Sirein: (coming soon)

Ragoru Beginnings Romance
White: Emala's Story
Huntress

Dark Spirits
Havoc of Souls
The Mirror (also part of Mischief Matchmakers)
Forest of Spirits
Desert of the Vanished (coming soon)

Shadowed Dreams Erotica
The Lantern
Serpent of the Abyss

The Mintars
Librarian and the Beast

The Atlavans

The Darvel Exploratory Systems
Classified Planet: Turongal

Argurma Salvager
Broken Earth
Pirate's Gold

ABOUT THE AUTHOR

S.J. Sanders is a writer of Science Fiction and Fantasy Romance. With a love of all things alien and monster she is fascinated with concepts of far off worlds, as well as the lore and legends of various cultures. When not writing, she loves reading, sculpting, painting and travel (especially to exotic destinations). Although born and raised in Alaska, she currently as a resident of Florida with her family, her maine coon, Bella, and pet bearded dragon, Lex.

Readers can follow her on Facebook:

https://www.facebook.com/authorsjsanders

Or join her Facebook group S.J. Sanders Unusual Playhouse

https://www.facebook.com/groups/361374411254067/

Newsletter:

https://mailchi.mp/7144ec4ca0e4/sjsandersromance
Website:

https://sjsandersromance.wordpress.com/